CONSPIRACY
of SILENCE

WESLEY MILTON LEE

Copyright © 2023 Wesley Milton Lee.

All rights reserved. No part of this book may be reproduced, stored, or transmitted by any means—whether auditory, graphic, mechanical, or electronic—without written permission of both publisher and author, except in the case of brief excerpts used in critical articles and reviews. Unauthorized reproduction of any part of this work is illegal and is punishable by law.

ISBN: 979-8-88640-794-5 (sc)
ISBN: 979-8-88640-795-2 (hc)
ISBN: 979-8-88640-796-9 (e)

Because of the dynamic nature of the Internet, any web addresses or links contained in this book may have changed since publication and may no longer be valid. The views expressed in this work are solely those of the author and do not necessarily reflect the views of the publisher, and the publisher hereby disclaims any responsibility for them.

One Galleria Blvd., Suite 1900, Metairie, LA 70001
1-888-421-2397

Three full decades had passed before I fully faced the fact I was born into some unusual dysfunction and my birth mother brought me up exactly like a child she never wanted, but after observation, understanding and being blessed with some total recall, it is what it is. I was born on May 15, 1968 in Norfolk, Virginia. My earliest childhood memories come from being brought up in the Calvert Park Housing Project in Norfolk. I was born the youngest of five children, each of us having a different father…six parents and five children. My mother was a very attractive woman…fair skinned, light complected, a shapely figure, and a pretty face. Those characteristics were often received with favor when I was growing up in the 70's. I know having children by five different men affected her mentally as well as emotionally. My oldest brother resembled my mother the most with the light skin and facial features. My oldest sister had the facial features of my mother, but she had a much darker complexion. My older sister was darker than my mother as well, but not as dark as my oldest sister, and her facial features didn't resemble my mothers'. My older brother also had a light complexion, but his facial features didn't resemble those of my mother or my oldest brother. Now comes me with a complexion and facial features like my oldest sister. We were all obviously different in physical appearance and we were brought up that way as well. We weren't brought up as a family, but as individuals…each according to our mothers' perception of us as individuals. This was a 'divide and conquer' tactic in the household. I was close to ten years younger than my oldest brother and all I saw him do was whatever he wanted. He randomly fought with my sisters and my older brother physically, and for no apparent reason. My mother never disciplined him for his actions, and he took full advantage of the fact. I recall me and my older brother laughing in the upstairs bedroom we slept in, and he told our mother to tell us to be quiet. She came into the room and said "Y'all be quiet". My initial thought was how the son could be telling the mother what to do, but I had to acknowledge what I observed. I don't know how either of my sisters' relationship with my mother was, but I never saw her being especially nice to either of them. I do recall my mother telling my older sister that she was beginning to resemble my oldest sister as if it was something negative. I noticed that my older sister began to get into cosmetics a little more, which is something I had never seen my oldest sister do. As for my older brother, having the same mother was simply a fact of the matter. I never felt any bond between us simply because he never put any brotherly characteristics on display. I recall going out on the back porch where he was talking to a neighbor. I went outside where they were and the neighbor asked me if I was afraid of my oldest brother and when I replied "no", my older brother said, "You sure act like it." I don't know what he was going by with that remark, but what came to my mind was the fact that he was regularly being punched on by our oldest brother and I wasn't. How he translated that to me being afraid of our oldest brother is beyond me. I was about nine years old when I jumped on my oldest brother's back to stop him from hitting on my older brother. My older brother said nothing about that. Any brotherly interactions I had with my older brother were always initiated by me. I recall my mother telling him to take me with him to one of his friends' houses who happened to have a brother my age and I saw the look on his face as if he didn't want to. She said to him, "I know." He didn't say anything on the way there or back home. With all of this in house division none of us would get together and wonder aloud about our home life. I knew back then that she could barely stand to hear her name called by any of us besides my oldest brother, let alone be questioned. When there are more parents than children, there are more questions than answers. I was basically ignored then, insignificant in retrospect. I had the most interactions with my oldest sister. I was in her care as far back as I can remember, since I was the only one in the house who couldn't take care of myself. With five children, my mother was still doing what she wanted to do outside of the house, also inside. I saw different men come into the house and leave without really interacting with me or my siblings. They went upstairs with my mother to her room. My father came over sometimes and talked with me. I recall him telling us to go outside and my mother didn't say anything. We were in the house almost all the time, except for my oldest brother. I don't have many memories of my father besides one time he took me to a department store and told me to pick out whatever I wanted. I picked out one toy. He also took me to his house to stay the night. I remember lying in bed staring at the ceiling and hearing my father say to my stepmother "What's wrong with him?" and her reply was "He's alright." One day my mother told me "C'mon" and we walked to my grandmothers' house…my father's mother. She didn't say a word on the way, and when we got inside my grandmother said to me "Your daddy is dead." I instinctively started crying and ran to my mother and I noticed neither of them were crying. I was six years old then and it was ruled an intravenous drug overdose. When we got back home, I noticed the expressions on the faces of my mother and my oldest brother. My oldest sister asked my mother if anyone knew what happened and my mother replied that my stepmother had paid someone to put salt water in my fathers' needle, but I didn't know what that meant. Even back then it was as if they knew something no one else did. Later in life I heard a few stories implicating my mother, but I wasn't there when whatever happened, and I had no one that I could go to for the purpose of even entertaining any curiosities I had back then. The things my mother told me about my father were basically about his alcohol consumption and that he was inebriated when I was conceived. She also told me about his way with a lot of women, and even mentioned her sister as one of them. She told me that she thought about killing him and contemplating an attempt to paralyze him by hitting him in the back. I heard from my oldest brother that my father attempted to get physical custody of me, but my mother fought it and won. My oldest sister told me that my father promised my mother he would marry her in a letter from jail, but he married my stepmother after he got out. My mother told me that my father came to the hospital and named me after him when I was born, and I had both of their last names. She told me that there was a name she already had in mind for me, which was 'Trent', and when I asked her who he was she said, "A friend of your father." Back then that was very confusing. I remember 'James', who was married to my grandmother on my mothers' side, telling me more than a few times "Your momma is mad about your daddy." I couldn't put that together back then. My earliest memories of her were not pleasant. I recall being very young and laying on my back, possibly to be changed when I feel pain from the tip of my penis being pinched, and I see my mothers' head come up in front of me at my feet. She was smiling in my face while I was feeling pain. I believe it's at least one of the reasons I had enuresis for a good part of my young life. I didn't know that pissing in the bed was a sign of abuse back then, but I do recall my mother saying aloud about me "There's something wrong with him." She was spanking me across her knee for pissing on myself in the presence of her male company and I bit her on the thigh. She kneed me off her lap onto the floor and I got up and ran to my oldest sister crying. I guess that I was with my oldest sister so much that I thought she was my mother. I called her mama and she said, "I'm not your mama, that's your mama." while pointing to my mother. When I called my mother mama she said, "Don't call me mama." Those words were the foundation of our relationship. I also recall a time when I was still very young, and my mother and I were in the house alone; it was already dark outside and she walked me into the pantry, turned off the lights, and screamed loud as hell directly into my ear. I stood there silent, and my mother had a look of disgust on her face. She just walked out of the pantry, and I became emotionally numb for the most part because I didn't know what she anticipated my reaction would be; she was upset at something I didn't do without me knowing what it was. Her facial expressions alone created an emotional distance between us because they were always hard. Many times, I wondered 'what did I do?' Her mother came to visit back then, and she had the same expression on her face when she looked at me as my mother did. My mother let me go with her to a department store by the name of J.M. Fields and she went there to shoplift, which I didn't know at the time. She was caught and I went up some stairs with her while she was going through the process. She was released and we rode back home, but the thing I remember the most is the whole time she never said a word to me, but when we got back to the house, she explained the entire scenario to my oldest brother in full detail. I was with my mother once when she went to a barbershop. We went in and I sat in one of the chairs for customers, but my mother went in some room in the back with one of the barbers. I sat there long enough to teach myself how to read backwards. 's'yrreJ' was the name of the barbershop. I was starting to think I might get a haircut when my mother came out from the back. She looked at me and said "C'mon." The barber had a smile on his face though. I paid attention to other families when I could, and how other mothers interacted with their children. What I saw looking at other families was the rule, but what I was experiencing at home was the exception to the rule. I recall her washing me up at the sink while keeping me at arm's length, and that look of disgust was always present. From her I was either ignored, belittled, or browbeaten at a very young age. Most of these experiences occurred before I was in kindergarten. The unconditional love that's assumed all mothers give totally missed me. I was dealt with indirectly and our interactions occurred only when they couldn't be avoided. Only in the presence of unknowing outsiders did she appear to like me, but she would revert to being her mean and neglectful self once they were no longer around. It was very confusing to me, and I began to see that neither of my siblings had to be obligated to me more than my mother should have been. My oldest brother would interact with me occasionally, and I guess it was alright just to be getting some attention. I saw how mean he would be towards our other siblings and back then I asked myself "Why doesn't he mess with me?" When I was around six years old, he started telling me this story about a man getting fucked in the ass by the devil. He brought that story up periodically for what seemed like a span of two to three months and never brought it up again. Around that time, I began having a memory, and it's a memory I can't fully retrieve because in the memory my eyes are closed. In this memory there's something in my mouth and whatever it is, is moving around. This memory stayed with me long after it began, and I recall bringing it up to my mother some years later. She didn't respond. My brothers and I slept three to a bedroom and sometimes my oldest brother would have people he associated with spend the night over. Those times my mother would have me sleep in her room on the floor. After long thought I realized that my mothers' bed was strictly reserved for her and her lovers only, and at a very young age I was being put in a position to accept the way that she would deal with me as her youngest child. The first time or one the first times this occurred, I awoke in the middle of the night and looked up to see a female image that was all white, with a dress down to the floor and I put my face down, hoping it would disappear, but when I looked back up it was still there. I did this at least two more times while looking in different directions and the image was still there. Finally, I put my face down to the floor and kept it there for the rest of the night. I didn't see it again and I told my mother about it the next morning and I know at least my oldest sister heard about it, but it was basically dismissed. I was too young to understand back then, but now I know that the image that I saw was an angel looking over me. There was another time when I was in her room asleep on the floor when my oldest brother came in and woke me out of my sleep. He said "Here Wesley " while he was showing his penis and I became afraid and hid under the bed for a long time. A while later he came back into the room and said "I ain't gon' mess with you no more". I still waited for some time before I came out of the room, and when I was going downstairs, he came to me and said "I'm sorry. Don't tell anybody, hear?" I never mentioned it...partly because of the way my mother dealt with me and the fact that I never saw my mother hold my oldest brother accountable for any wrong he did. Later in life I often wondered why he would do some shit like that seemingly 'out of the blue'. I saw my mother and my oldest brother express their differences verbally and they both used the same amount of profanity. I recall an argument they were having on one occasion when she got a butcher knife out of the drawer and was going towards him. He looked directly at her and said, "What do you want to kill me for?" They both looked at me, and my mother put the knife away. I was intimidated by the loud yelling and screaming I often heard, which was mostly by my mother and my oldest brother, but I began to be mindful of what was said before either of them stopped talking. With four younger siblings my oldest brother had the advantages of an only child. He had his favorite cereal 'Count Chocula' which was off limits to the rest of us and he would have all the paint he needed to put on the uniforms of the teams he had to play electronic football. He would sometimes wake me in the middle of the night to talk about things my mind wasn't ready to process, and other times he would wake me and walk me downstairs to my sisters' bedroom and rub between their legs while they were sleeping. I don't know if my mother knew what he was doing, but I know she was aware of what he was capable of. My mother was at home during the day back then, usually lashing out in profanity laced tirades that were not specifically directed towards anyone, but I once heard my oldest brother say "She ain't talking to me." I soon realized after hearing that; I was the only one listening to her. I recall going to an appointment at the Doctor's Office with my mother and my older brother, and the receptionist asked my mother the name of my older brothers' father. She gave the name of a man who had been coming to the house for parts of three decades. He called on the telephone for her back when I was younger and began to come over. He was basically there to see my mother, but a few times my older brother and I got to ride out with them...to the movies, the circus and a few other places. When he did come over, I never saw him and my older brother interact on a father-son-vibe. I do recall when we were leaving the Scope Arena and walking to this mans' car. I noticed how close my mother was to this man while they were walking, and I began to walk slower. Before too long, my mother called out to me, and I let her know that I wasn't far away. There was an incident when this man came over and I was about eight years old. He was sitting in the kitchen with my mother when she called me and my older brother in. She had two cups out for us and there was a six-pack of Budweiser on the table. She gave me my cup and was smiling at me. She had never smiled at me before, but it was a welcome sight. I drank it down, and it was Budweiser. I don't know if she gave my older brother anything, but I do recall this man leaving the house and my mother walking him to the door smiling all the way, but when she closed the door after he was gone the expression on her face was all but...I saw her display that behavior from more men than him. Home life with my mother in the house was my elementary school reality. My older siblings went out and came in, but I was in the house watching my mother watch TV. She watched 'Gunsmoke' and 'The Rifleman' along with 'The Big Valley' and 'Bonanza'. 'Perry Mason' was one of her favorites, but while we were in the room together, she didn't look my way or even say a word to me unless I got up to leave the room. She rarely spoke with me and for some reason I began to pay more attention to her mannerisms. I realized that when she talked to me it was as if she knew all the things I didn't. I also noticed that she never gave direct answers. There were either sarcastic responses, lip smacking or negative facial expressions. I found two words to describe her ways when it came to how she dealt with me, and they were condescending and equivocal. I recall her telling me that I was 'sorry' on more than a few occasions and also she told me that in her words "I ain't gon' tell you nuthin'...you gon' do what you gon' do anyway". I saw it as her justifying being neglectful towards me, and she never called me by my name back then; I was called 'Little One'. She talked with my oldest brother as if they were on the same level, and they often talked down on the rest of us with one another. She gave my older brother what I call 'secret love' simply by allowing his father in her house, but not directly in his son's life. I'm thankful for being good at school and always being at the top of my class as far as grades go. I always had the biggest lunch on field trips which definitely wouldn't raise any suspicion by any school faculty members. I was still pissin' in the bed at night and a lot of times I pissed on myself at school by just being afraid to ask to go to the restroom. I would be sitting at the kitchen table doing homework when my mother came home, and when she saw me she would go straight upstairs to her room without saying a word. There were times when I called her name or knocked on her bedroom door and the response would always be an emphatic "What!?" A few times she caught herself in the midst of her anger and lowered her voice, but the expression on her face still matched her initial response. My siblings were basically doing their own thing and that's just how it was. My mother kept me at an emotional distance to the point that I didn't even know how to approach her. I was always getting the best grades in elementary school, but it was as if I could do nothing right at home because my mother didn't hesitate to let me know when I did or didn't do something that was wrong in her eyes. There were times when my mother sat in a chair on the front porch with me in her lap, and I would see boys my age that I went to school with walking by independently and it gave me mixed emotions back then simply because of the lack of attention she gave me inside the house. My siblings would be that way towards me at times, but never my older sister. She never talked to me in a negative way. I was never given any advice or told anything for my own good, but if I did something wrong I would definitely hear about it from someone in the family. "And you're supposed to be the smart one." was a phrase I often heard back then. Being smart in school was met with indifference in the household, and possibly some resentment due to the fact that I earned those grades in the classroom and I never had help doing my homework. There was nothing I could do about being basically overlooked at home. I recall a time when I was in the upstairs front bedroom with my mother and my oldest sister. My mother was looking out the window and said "That's a cute little boy." She was actually referring to a boy about my same age and the realization of it was confusing simply because she was smiling at a boy outside the window and regularly looked down on me inside the house. Being ignored on a daily basis eventually enabled me to remember just about everything I had seen or heard in the household. Being left-handed, I took what I heard literally and made it a point to remember whatever I had seen. I do recall my older brother saying that it looks like I'm doing everything wrong in reference to me being left-handed, but my oldest brother was left-handed as well. I was very much an introvert in school because I wasn't sure how to approach people or interact with them. When I was in the first grade I actually began reading the book of 'Genesis' in the Holy Bible. I liked to read, and did it often. I also began to watch television when no one else was around. I never embraced being disregarded, but since it was that way I had no choice but to accept it. I was getting used to it without really understanding it. Around the time I was eight or nine years old my oldest sister told me that my mother jumped off of a porch when she was nine months pregnant with me, and my mother was present when she said it. When I looked at my mother she didn't say a word, but I knew that the porch was at least three feet high off the ground. Looking back, I'm convinced it was an attempt to terminate her pregnancy simply by the way she treated me, but to put her own life at risk with such an attempt is something I can't explain. When I was in the fourth grade my oldest brother was up in our bedroom with a girl and he called me upstairs and said "Do you want some pussy?" I told him no and went back downstairs, but I thought about it for a long time afterwards. When I look back on it I believe he was trying to erase something he was guilty for while also attempting to get an angle on my sexual preference. I can also recall an incident when I was passing by my mothers' bedroom on my way to the bathroom. There was a man in the room with her and the door was open somewhat, but when she noticed me walking by she leaned across the bed towards me with her lips puckered up while she was still partially under the covers. I simply backed away and proceeded to the bathroom. This was around the same time when my mother went to get ski coats for my older brother and me. She had a normal coat for my older brother with elastic around the waist and wrists, but she got me one that was made for a girl. She said that she couldn't find a boys' coat in my size and I was confused because I didn't have another coat. Her final words on the matter were "Ain't nobody gonna say nothing." In the second grade I began wearing eyeglasses and I also broke a few pairs, but as I got a little older and looked at some of my old school pictures I noticed that some of my eyeglasses had female frames. My oldest sister had a baby boy when I was in the third grade and everyone seemed to be happy about it except for my oldest brother, possibly because it diverted some of my mothers' attention away from him. The baby passed away from SIDS at six weeks old and I was devastated, simply because I didn't understand how things like that could or would happen. His life briefly provided us with a sense of family unity. This was during a period when my oldest brother began spending time in jail for one thing or another. I recall watching him at the kitchen table with a bottle of five hundred saccharin pills and two 'Magic Markers'; one orange and the other purple. He colored each pill with the intent of selling them for three dollars each. I could easily calculate that up and I knew it was illegal in some sort of way, but that was the privilege he had in the house. Things were peaceful around the house when he wasn't there simply because he was so antagonistic towards the other siblings. My mother once made a remark in regards to him being locked up if something went awry in the house. "Y'all can't put it on him" was what she said. My older sister would regularly spend her summer vacation in Maryland with our grandmother. In retrospect, I'm glad she had an out because my oldest brother was so mean to her for no apparent reason and our mother never defended her against him. I had an especially memorable Christmas at the age of ten; no tree, gifts or dinner. My mother was up in her bedroom with the door closed and my older brother and I were in the kitchen. There was no milk and I was eating dry 'Raisin Bran' from a bowl. I started to choke and my life was flashing before my face. My older brother reacted quickly by using the 'Heimlich Maneuver' to stop me from choking, but I was so traumatized that I couldn't stop crying. My mother came almost all the way down the steps to see what was wrong and when my older brother told her that I was choking, she looked at me shortly and went back upstairs to her bedroom. That incident was brought back up a while later at the kitchen table while my sisters were present, and I was crying again at the thought of it. My mother was looking at me as if she was somehow disappointed, but she never said a word. Neither did anyone else. The dysfunction continued, and when I was promoted to the sixth grade I had to go to a different school in Tidewater Park; still not knowing how to interact with people outside of the house because I didn't know how to interact in the house with my family. I had absolutely no confidence in myself, but I relied on my book smarts and recognized when it was time to be quiet around people I didn't really know. My oldest brother was receiving enough special attention from our mother to the point that he had courage and confidence; there was nothing he couldn't do or get away with in his mind simply because she always supported him openly. Fellas respected or feared him and females liked him. My older brother would often break character or overdo it to gain acceptance from his peers to the point that he would often belittle me in front of them without fully understanding that they had younger brothers who were around my age, and who were probably more socially advanced than he was. He would entertain me and my peers at times and I believe he thought that he could influence me, as well as them simply because he was older. I had always shown respect to him openly, but I always paid attention to the way that he portrayed himself in general. Around that time there was an incident when my mother, my brothers and I were in the kitchen eating corned beef hash and pork n beans. My mother began to fix dinner less and less. I was the only one in the house who was going to school on a regular basis, but getting a decent meal depended on how she felt. I got no special favors and if she didn't feel like putting a meal together, or if the cupboard was bare, I had to fend for myself. There was a knock at the door and my oldest brother answered it. He came back into the kitchen and said to me "There's about fifteen girls at the door for you!" I said "I ain't goin' out there!", and my oldest brother said "You better go ahead boy!" When I went to the door there were fifteen girls from my new school standing outside. I went out to talk with them, but I was clearly outnumbered so I went down my row and knocked on the door of some of my peers to try and balance the situation. I rounded up about five fellas, and we all walked and talked together like we were grownups. I don't recall how long we hung out, but when I went back home I realized that my older brother never came outside, not even out of curiosity. I felt a way about that, but I couldn't put it together. I never asked him about it. The females began to come through on a regular basis, especially to play 'spin the bottle' in front of a house right behind where I lived. I recall one occasion when my older brother was there and I encouraged him to participate, but he showed no interest at all. When I got to junior high school things were basically the same as far as my home life was, but I began to understand things about it better. When I was in the seventh grade my mother put me on punishment for having a bad report card and besides school I couldn't leave the house for nine weeks. The thing about it is the fact that everyone was still living at home for the most part, and no one there finished school. Being in the house for such a long period of time, I eventually became overweight. I was already an introvert, but I became self-conscious as well. I heard my share of 'fat jokes' from outsiders as well as family. I began losing focus on getting good grades; being intelligent didn't seem to matter as much, because my home life was my reality. Love was never expressed; only negativity, or good moods sometimes. I didn't like how it was and I couldn't survive on my own. I didn't have an out, but I paid attention to the adults who came by back then and how they interacted with my mother, and to me it seemed as if they looked at her as if she was a victim in some kind of way, even my grandmother on my fathers' side. Around that time I watched my oldest brother begin making imitation hashish to sell to people. He would mix it up and bake it in the oven, and it had an awful smell. He would have people in the house to smoke real hashish he had, but he would sell them the stuff he made. He was also selling marijuana out of the house, and different people were coming by at random times of the day and night. My mother was aware of all of this, but it wasn't anything more than that. Around that time I was selected to attend an enrichment program called 'Discovery 81' at Virginia Wesleyan College for students with high IQs. My IQ was '137' in the sixth grade, but I'm sure that it had risen by then. My mother came up with the money for me to be able to go, and I was thankful for that. The program lasted for two weeks and it was very enlightening. We stayed in dormitories and we had to do our own laundry. There were one hundred students selected, and ten of us were black; seven girls and three boys; I made sure I was mindful of that fact. When it was over and I went back home the realities were still there, but I began to understand that I wrongly assumed that the family I was born into would automatically show me unconditional love. Everyone in the house was following their own path, and no unity was present. My older sister had a baby boy around this time, and I simply recall how my mother looked at him. It was with such disdain, like how her mother looked at me. There was an incident when I was looking at him the same way that I saw my mother look at him, and my older brother saw me. He said "You're just like your mama." It hit me immediately because he was right as far as me doing what I had seen my mother constantly do, but I never believed that I had any of her characteristics. It made me understand that I was once in that same situation as a young child; possibly before I could remember, but I showed love to every child that came into the family after me. I could not control the discord that was being sown by other family members, but I was not going to continue the cycle of dysfunction. I was among a select few students who were selected to go to Norfolk State University to take a PSAT test. I was in junior high school sitting with college students, which seemed pretty awkward, but I held my own as far as my scores were concerned. I was beginning to believe that I could use my intelligence to somehow bring my family up into a more favorable position, but those ideas were never reinforced in the home. The differences of my family members were becoming more apparent; maybe the personalities of all our fathers were beginning to surface. My oldest brother would have company over all night at times, and so did my oldest sister. When this happened I had to sleep on the floor in my mothers' room. On one occasion my oldest brother took issue with my oldest sisters' company and a fight ensued. My oldest brother stabbed him in the wrist with a steak knife. There was another time when my oldest brother and sister were fighting each other. He hit her in the head with a table leg, giving her a concussion and she sliced him across the stomach with a kitchen knife. After she cut him he shouted out to our mother "look what she did to me!" A neighbor gave aid to my oldest sister, but my mother took my oldest brother to the emergency room. I had never seen any issues go that far, but the open differences occurred on a regular basis. I saw my oldest brother get into confrontations with friends of my older brother, disregarding the fact that he was an adult and they were juveniles. One time I was sitting in the kitchen and I noticed one of my neighbors running down the steps and out the front door. My older brother told me that my oldest brother punched him in the face while they were upstairs. When I witnessed my oldest brother behave in that manner, it was as if he was constantly trying to establish some type of dominance over those around him. When our mother was present she never intervened, not even when he was physically assaulting a female in the living room. I recall the woman screaming out "You all act like you're scared of him!", but I had always felt like it was up to our mother to make the first move in those kinds of situations simply because she had the position of matriarch. My oldest brother and this woman eventually got married and she moved to Kansas. Around that time I can remember the phone bill going upwards of a thousand dollars because of my oldest brother. That situation was a big deal to me, but it seemed as if my mother let it ride. I don't believe anyone in the house was working at that time, but the bill got paid after a good while. I don't know how it got paid, but I was damn near certain that they had some secrets on one another, because I never saw him face any repercussions from our mother about any of his wrongdoings. I began receiving Social Security checks around that time for something pertaining to my father. The checks came in my mothers' name, and the first one was around thirteen hundred dollars. They would come monthly as long as I was enrolled in school. Also, not every check was as much as the first one. My mother took me to cash the first check and bought me some summer outfits. She spent a decent amount of money, but there was still plenty left. She put the remaining money in my hands without giving me any financial advice or telling me what bills I could help pay. She literally said nothing, and neither did I. That's how it was whenever those checks came. I would look out for my older brother with what I could simply because it was a way to help. He accepted what I could do, but not openly. I was beginning to understand that being a middle brother wasn't easy for him due to the fact that our oldest brother would antagonize him without warning and seemingly for no reason at all, but I was always loyal to him. Our mother was beginning to openly belittle me in his presence for whatever reason, and it seemed as if he was starting to look at me through her eyes. We had no personal business with one another and really didn't vibe with each other. That was confusing to me, but whenever I was outside my peers seemed to gravitate towards me. When I started high school I always felt that being intelligent would be enough to get through, but as the end of the school day neared I had already begun to wonder about what different experience I would have to encounter once I got home. I was getting more positive attention from outside the house than inside. My older sister had moved out of the house around that time and my oldest brother had gotten married and was living in Kansas. My mother had resurrected her love life and the disdain that I had been constantly receiving from her had lessened to a degree. She began to buy furniture for the living room and put a large table in the downstairs bedroom. My oldest sister became pregnant again and we actually had to sleep in a twin bed together at times. I felt like if any of the grown children had to come back home, there would not be any comfort involved. By the time I had completed my second year of high school I had grown to six feet tall and my weight stretched up instead of out. I was the tallest one in the family and the attention I had received from the females prior to me becoming a teenager was coming back. I was also getting more open respect from the guys around my age. School wasn't hard at all, and the thought of me being the first one in the family to graduate from high school began to surface. Some of my classmates and teachers as well were openly acknowledging to me the potential they felt that I had, but I received none of that at home. There was no encouragement, building or uplifting inside the house, but if I did anything that could be considered negative I would definitely hear about it. If my mother was in a good mood she would smile at me sometimes, but that was usually when she had male company around. There was an incident when I had come into the house about the same time the man who my mother said was the father of my older brother was getting ready to leave. After he left my mother confronted me and said with anger "He said he might not come back." as if there was something I had done to prompt him to say that to her. My understanding of my home life was becoming more clear, but I didn't like it at all. I could easily tell that my older brother felt better about himself when I was overweight, but once I became taller than him the little interaction we did have with each other was occurring less and less. I recall our mother saying to him back then "If you can't say anything nice, don't say anything at all. The fact of the matter was that neither of them would ever say anything nice to me at all. Once again the girls were knocking at the door for me on a regular basis and I would summon any of the guys I knew to help balance the male to female ratio. If my older brother was around, his inadequacies around females became present when he chose to express himself. There were times when he would comment to me about the things that wasn't doing when it came to the females, but up to that point I could only recall him having one summer love. He told me stories about his female conquests, and I'm pretty sure that was all they were because no girls ever came to the house looking for him. According to him, he was having sex with a female at her house and her parents came in the bedroom. He said that they both apologized, left out of the room and closed the door behind them. We have a three year age difference between us and I was about thirteen years old at the time. I could not disprove his words, but that story never made sense to me. Those kinds of stories often came out of the blue without warning and had very little detail. They just happened. Around that time my oldest brothers' marriage was over and he was back at the house. Shortly after, both my brothers went out of town where my older sister was and found employment for a brief time. They both came back home before the summer was over and old memories were beginning to resurface. My oldest brother began selling cocaine from the house and people were coming by all times of day and night. Getting a good night's sleep for school was becoming next to impossible. My oldest brother had an outright issue without mothers' love interest at the time, and to me it seemed as if his anger bordered on jealousy. He told her things about that man in an attempt to get her to stop dealing with him, but that wasn't going to work. This struck me funny because as far back as I could recall, my mother and my oldest brother always liked and disliked the same people, with one exception. My mother didn't like me while my oldest brother acted like he did, and she acted as if she liked my older brother while my oldest brother didn't. An incident occurred around that time when I was playing sandlot football. I gave a guy a serious blow on a busted play and knocked him to the ground, but after he got up he walked towards me and swung on me. I grabbed him and we both went to the ground. My oldest brother ran out to the field and kicked the guy in the mouth. He was grown and the rest of us were juveniles, so he took a real chance doing that. My older brother was on the sideline watching the game as well. When we got home I asked my older brother if he would help me out while I was in a fight and his reply to me was "Not if it's one on one." He gave an honest answer but I don't think he knew that he wasn't supposed to say that. The guy was bigger than I was and that didn't mean much, but on another occasion prior to that incident, I was playing football and another guy clipped me while I was running. I got up and started chasing him. He was smaller and faster than I was, and I couldn't catch him. My older brother grabbed him and held him for me, and my older brother was also the biggest one out there at the time. All of the kids playing were much younger and smaller than he was. Those two incidents didn't match up. One time my high school locker was broken into and a jacket and hat belonging to me was stolen. I found out who it was, and I had plans to confront the person responsible later that evening at the dance. Time was approaching so I left the house and went on my way, but I noticed my older brother coming behind me. He just started walking beside me and didn't say anything the whole time we were walking. It wasn't long after he made that 'not if it's one on one' comment, and I believed that the situation was brought up again. I'm pretty sure that our mother put him up to going with me because I was caught off guard by it. His brotherly loyalty, or lack thereof, was quite obvious to me by that time. I was often angry when I was in the house for the simple fact that my mother was methodically turning my older brother against me, and as long as he was getting any favor over me or was made to appear better than me in any capacity, he would go right along with it. By the end of my third year in high school my oldest brother had developed an addiction to heroin, and my oldest sister had moved into a house around the corner, and by that time she had a son and a daughter. My older brother shared the house with her and it was definitely a getaway for me at times. I took her son under my wing and began to take him with me to places I would go. There was an incident when he was acting up in the presence of my mother and my oldest sister. He happened to have a toy gun in his hand, and when I yelled at him, he pointed the gun at me and pulled the trigger. My mother was all too amused by that and began to laugh loudly, but my oldest sister didn't say anything. That's how my mother felt about that situation, but I would take my nephew with me to let him experience something other than gossip and manipulation. I came into the house one night from playing basketball, and my mother was cooking dinner. When I got into the kitchen I said I've worked up an appetite." My mother quickly responded "Now go back out there and work it off." This was a normal thing coming from her, but the older I became the more it pissed me off. I went back outside to let my anger subside, and when I came back in she acted like she had an attitude with me. She knew how to wipe a smile off of my face, and didn't have any problem doing it. I didn't pay it as much mind when I was younger, but I realized that she was doing it intentionally, and who was around when she did it mattered less and less. She became close with one of the neighbors who was the same age as my older brother, and they were actually childhood friends until my older brother was told that this person was gay. My mother brought this to my attention after not talking to me on purpose for the longest durations of time. She said "Your brother stopped walking to school with that boy just because the other boys said he was a faggot." In my mind I was wondering what the hell she was telling me for, but as they became closer, she would openly insult me in his presence, and he would laugh every time. She was still carrying it with me as if I was supposed to do something to make her happy, but she never said what it was. By that time my negative home experiences had far outweighed the positive ones. She had someone go to the store around that time to get a six-pack of some new malt liquor that had come out. She encouraged my older brother and I to try it. I don't know what my brother did, but I drank what was given to me. The way I felt from drinking it made tolerating home life seem easier. I watched, listened and became more honest with myself. My oldest brother was strung out on heroin and would go on binges for days at a time, wearing my school clothes. I didn't know if I wanted them back or not, but my mother didn't say or do anything about it on my behalf. He would often sell fake drugs to people, knowing that they knew where he lived. They would often come back to the house looking for retaliation. On one particular occasion a guy was running after my oldest brother with an axe, swinging it at him. There would be times when I would come home from school and he would have junkies all in the house. They would be shooting drugs, and a few times I saw blood in the bathroom sink. I had a summer job around that time, and late one night he came into the bedroom, waking me out of my sleep. He told me that he owed somebody money and that person said that he would shoot the next person that walked out of our house. I gave him the money without really knowing whether he was telling the truth or not. My mother looked at any mistake that I made as the worst thing that could ever happen, and she didn't look at the things he did on purpose at all. I saw no sense in telling her things about my oldest brother because she already knew. One day around that time I was riding a skateboard and an older woman, possibly around my mothers' age, was driving up behind me in a school bus, yelling at me through the window. She was accusing me of messing with her daughter and I was trying to make it to the curb. I went directly home and told my mother. Her response was "Let her bring her fat ass over here." I could only think about the numerous times that she literally ran out of the house in my oldest brothers' defense, and would fight his battles. I remember walking to the store and a car pulling up on me. When the car stopped, an old schoolmate of mine jumped out with a .38 revolver in his hand. He was accusing me of wanting to bring harm to him in some type of way. It didn't take long for a crowd to gather around, there were people yelling "Don't kill him!" I just stood still and silent. The situation calmed down after a while and he got back into the car and pulled off. I went back home and never mentioned it to anyone. Around that time my maternal grandmother had passed away. She was in Maryland, and we drove there for the funeral. I got to see my older sister and her son my nephew while we were there, and when we were all dressed for the funeral my older sister complimented me on how I looked in a suit, but I couldn't help but notice the look on my older brothers' face when he heard it. He definitely craved attention, and whenever he saw me getting any I could tell that he felt a certain way about it. That came from wanting to believe all the negative things he heard our mother say about me. One day I came home from school and my mother was in the kitchen washing dishes. When she saw that it was me, she just turned back around. With her back to me she openly suggested that I try to be like our next door neighbor. I was instantly pissed off because I was feeling good about myself in spite of my home life. The neighbor that she was referring to was gay, and even if he hadn't been, that was far from unconditional love coming from a mother. There was another time that I came into the house while she was washing dishes, and once again she turned around immediately when she saw that it was me. With her back to me she asked if my oldest brother had talked me into using drugs. Nothing like that was going on, but she was basically excusing herself from any responsibility regarding the matter. Her frequent antagonistic ways towards me signified that she was trying to provoke a certain reaction from me. I recall when I was approaching junior high school, my mother allowed me to pick two magazines to subscribe to. One of them was called 'Games' and there were all different kinds of puzzles in those magazines that tested a persons' problem solving and critical thinking ability. Being alone most of the time back then I couldn't wait for one of those magazines to come in the mail. I would try to solve most of the puzzles in every magazine I got, and was better at some than at others. Being left handed did a lot of good for my lateral thinking. I was beginning to figure things out without a lot of information to go on, simply by observing and assessing a situation. It helped me in school, and it gave me a better understanding of the family that I was born into. The less time we spent together, the better we got along. My sisters were basically looking at things the way our mother did, and she totally accepted whatever my oldest brother did, even though the things he was doing were obviously wrong. She knew that was a situation that couldn't be rectified, and the guilt that she would never openly show led her to one last divisive maneuver; outwardly favor my older brother against me. He often interpreted her verbal abuse towards me as a compliment to himself without realizing that a person has to earn their own merit. The negativity had filtered down to me, so I was in a situation where I had to look, listen and observe. There was a divide and conquer approach going on from a mother to her children. I was out playing basketball and an acquaintance of mine told me that he saw my oldest brother in court. The thing about it is that he told me that my brother had given the people my name for his case. By that time, my oldest sister had another son and I had a child on the way. When I told my mother her exact words were "Don't expect me to be crazy about him." And that's all she said to me on the subject, but some days later her love interest was in the house, and when he saw me he said "What you gonna do now daddy?" She wouldn't talk to me, but talking about me was no problem at all. Around that time I remember coming into the house and running upstairs, and when I reached the top of the stairs I could see my oldest brother standing in front of the mirror with a syringe in his arm. When he realized that I was looking at he started to push the door closed, but he turned the door loose and continued to do what he was doing. He would cross anyone to get what he wanted, and he was in and out of jail on a regular basis. Around late '87' my oldest brother called collect from jail, and when I accepted the call, he asked me for my Social Security Number. I told him I couldn't do that and then he asked me to try and get the Social Security Number of one of our nephews by my oldest sister. That didn't happen either. He already had my name downtown and was willing to let me take the charges for crimes he committed. He had been asking me to do wrong since I was very young, but as I look back, he was really telling me. I was about nine years old when he told me to bring a bag to him while was on the basketball court. There was a musket in the bag, and when I gave it to him, he packed the muzzle and fired it. On another occasion, I was walking from an event at Waterside when I heard him calling me from way behind, and as I was approaching him, I noticed he was carrying some white boxes and having a difficult time. They were boxes of frozen shrimp that he had taken, and he wanted me to help him carry them to the nightclub across the street. I remember when he broke into a car which happened to belong to a doctor, and he brought some of the contents in the house, which included a checkbook. I noticed that he was forging those checks for his own personal gain, and one day after I got home from school he came to me with a check in his hand and said "Sign this." We went back and forth about it for a few minutes, but I did it reluctantly. I couldn't be justified for doing it and I can't make excuses for myself. That next day, I didn't come directly home from school, and when I got there my mother was acting concerned as to my whereabouts. Apparently, my oldest brother told her that I signed one of the checks. By that time I realized that genuine concern constitutes more than a facial expression, and that issue was quickly dismissed. I was loyal to my family members to a fault, holding out hope that someone would change their ways. I was thankful to have a better understanding of them, but at some point I was looking too hard because I was beginning to repeat some of the things that I heard being said, and doing some of the things that I had seen done. Having a mother who literally couldn't stand the sight of my face was tough. My life was spiraling downward, and I stopped going to school two months before graduation. The answers to real life were not in clear view, but they definitely weren't in school. With no more SSI checks coming and a child on the way, my reality was becoming more real. I spent more and more time at my oldest sisters' house, playing cards, having selling parties and taking care of my niece and nephews when my sister had something to do. I was over there around late spring one evening and heard a knock at the door. When I opened the door, it was my mother, and all she said was "Where's my key?" I gave it to her, closed the door and went back inside. My oldest sister said "I can tell it's something by the look on your face." The way my mother dealt with me was nothing new, but I never liked it, and I figured by that time she was set in her ways or had made a conscious decision to stay how she was when it came to me. My oldest sister moved into an apartment after a while, and my older sister was back in town with a new baby girl. She and my older brother began sharing an apartment close by, but in a matter of months she went back to Maryland and left the apartment with my older brother. I stayed there at times, but I wasn't employed and my older brother eventually had to give it up. We both were back at the house with our mother. About spring '88' I came to the house early after spending the night out, and my mother was on the phone. I was about to keep going by until she handed the phone to me. It was my oldest brother on the phone from jail, and he was trying to give me a lecture about staying out all night. I noticed the expression on my mothers' face after she gave the phone to me. I detected more manipulation at work from her end. They both knew that she never gave a damn about me, but I guess that was as good a time as any to keep the lie alive. I fully knew that they were joined by lies and deceit. I considered the family that I was born into as enigmatic, with my mother and oldest brother leading the way. I was clearly the minority, simply by being the youngest of us all and I felt as if I was the only one of us who regularly put righteous principles on display. I listened to my oldest brother talk on the phone and gave it back to our mother after he finished talking. I didn't respond to anything he said and went about my business. When my oldest brother was in jail I visited him and took him clothes. I also gave him some poems that I had written. He was in the local jail, which was close to the house. He was moved further away around '91'. On one occasion, I was sitting at the kitchen table writing a poem and noticed my mother smiling at me. I asked her what she was smiling at and she said it made her think of my oldest brother when he used to draw. It wasn't about me at all; just a backhanded compliment. She had a trial to deal with when she was fired from her job for stealing money and failing a polygraph test. Listening to her talk about it, I got the impression that she would never admit to any wrongdoing, and probably never had. She still talked like she was spot free regardless of the obvious. A friend of mine helped me get a job at the lumberyard where he worked. I just felt good knowing when I woke up in the morning, I had something to do. My mother was working at a nearby convenience store around that time and I pitched in what I could, with my son to consider as well. Every time I gave her money, she would simply give me the low eye without responding. On one hand, I felt like I wasn't giving her enough, but on the other hand, I recall my oldest brother making stacks of money from inside the house and never giving her a dime; constantly putting the family at risk of getting evicted because of his illegal activities. By that time I had another child due at the beginning of '89'. That gave me good thoughts for the most part, and even though I had the same home life, I was less consumed by it. My mother was still using her influence to squash any harmony between my older brother and I. We mostly played basketball, drank alcohol and shared a few laughs together. Whenever we were in tune together in her presence, she would intervene by stepping in and giving me the low eye. Things would often become silent after that. My older brother and I were in the upstairs bedroom having a conversation when our mother came in and sarcastically interrupted me. I said to her "I wasn't talking to you." and she stepped to me, looking squarely in my eyes, chest to chest. When that happened, I looked at my brother and realized that had forced his hand. I was regularly trying to open his eyes about how wrong it was for a mother to treat her kids so differently, particularly him and me, and his only response was "She just shows me how not to be." I had never openly disrespected her or directed any anger towards her, and I believe she resented that. My older brother began working at the lumberyard shortly after I did and sometimes I would ride with him. He was living with a woman at the time, and that was the first time I can recall him being in a relationship. There would be days we would ride to work together and he would leave early without letting me know. I could only shake my head when it happened, knowing that his principles were non-existent. His woman called me one night and told me that he had an altercation at our oldest sisters' house. He told me there was a physical confrontation between him and our sisters' female roommate, and our sister as well. Not long after the incident, my brother noticed our sister and her roommate near the house and said "I'm going to get my hit back." He walked down to where they were with that intent, and I went to attempt to de-escalate the situation. They began arguing, and I was trying to hold him back, but he got close enough to take a swing at the roommate. While they were walking away, the roommate told my brother that she was going to have her brother shoot him. When I heard that I told my brother to walk with me. We went across the field to the house of an acquaintance of mine, and when we got there I asked him for a gun. He gave me a .25 revolver and we went back to the house. I gave him the gun and said "She threatened you and don't think she's bluffing just because our sister was with her." I had forgotten about it after that, but not even a month later I came into the house around midnight and went upstairs. When I got to the top of the stairs I noticed that my mothers' room door was half open, but I couldn't see her. What I did see was the gun I had given my older brother on the day he was threatened. I could only think she wanted to kill me and try to make it look like an accident. I went to the bathroom and went back downstairs. My brother must have given her the gun as soon as I gave it to him. I had plenty of suspicions about my mothers' mental state and one particular incident supported those suspicions further. I came in around eleven one night and was sitting at the kitchen table. While I was sitting there with a view of the stairway when I noticed my mother come down. She was wearing some open, see thru, Victoria's Secret type of shit on. I immediately put my head down until she went back upstairs, and when she did I could only say to myself "What the fuck is wrong with her?" I told my oldest sister about it and she responded as if it was nothing new to her, but I was a grown man seeing some shit like that for the first time. Around that time I got word that someone in the house where my sons were living was being threatened by a drug dealer. I was walking over there when I crossed paths with my older brother. I let him know what the situation was and after I was done talking, he proceeded to the house without saying a word. Protecting my sons was my main focus, but in retrospect this was another revelation. There are a handful of words which could be used to describe the behavior my older brother put on display in front of me, however, I'm not fit to judge. One time the rent was late, and the Housing Authority locked the doors on us as opposed to putting our things out in the street, supposedly because the furniture that my mother had in the house was 'too nice'. She had to stay with my oldest sister temporarily, and did so without a bit of humility. I was already spending plenty of time there, so it was nothing to me. I walked in my sisters' house one day around that time, and my mother and her were having a conversation about my older brother. My mother was calling him stupid in reference to the woman he was in a relationship with at the time. I told her to stop talking about people and she swung at me. I said it again and she swung at me again. My reasoning was that anyone in a predicament should concentrate on getting out of it, first and foremost. When I saw him I told him about it, and I believe he confronted our mother about it. I didn't see him for a few days after that, but the next time I did see him the first thing he said to me was "I stopped drinking." I knew then that our mother told him to say that to me because that was basically all we did together, but what made me sad about that situation was the fact my brother didn't realize he was being a victim of devious manipulation, or he didn't mind, and our mother would go to any length to keep a wedge between him and me. She was all we had in common besides our siblings by her. We looked different from one another, and our actions in certain situations would strongly suggest that we didn't think alike. The few times we were out together around people who didn't know us, it was always assumed that I was older. My oldest brother was in the midst of serving a long sentence and sometimes I rode the church bus to visit him. We exchanged letters often and I was regularly suggesting that he choose positivity over negativity, but I could tell he was still only out for what he could get. It was only me at the house with my mother at that time, and I made it my business to cross paths with her as little as possible. When I wasn't working I was spending time with my sons, and I came to the house to shower, sleep and change clothes. I quit my job at the lumberyard due to a petty difference and had another child on the way. Lack of steady employment was tough, but I did it to myself. I was working through agencies and temp services, but that was basically to make sure my sons had whatever they needed. My oldest sister had moved closer to the house in a neighboring public housing complex, and I often took my boys to her house so they could get acquainted with their cousins. Things seemed regular, but with my boys being so young I was constantly contemplating how I was going to become a full time provider when it came to them. Around '92' I was working two jobs and my fourth son was on the way. At the house, the most that I would hear from my mother was about how my work clothes smelled. None of that mattered because being a present and active father was my main objective. By the end of the summer I had lost both of my jobs and I was scrambling once again. Everyone was living their own lives and dealing with their own issues, but the fact that I had never received any genuine concern at all should not have come as a surprise to me. My mother had the dysfunction working in her favor, and pretty much everyone who knew the both of us looked at me through her eyes. I could only think back to my late teen years when a few of her acquaintances from work or whatever, expressed their curiosity about me to her. Neither instance lasted long at all, and I'm pretty sure she steered them away. I guess that could be called 'a mothers' influence'. Since I had been put in a position to accept everything that I had observed up to that point, I realized that any situation, problem or issue that I had, was mine. I had spent years around people who were mean spirited and selfish with nothing to gain. My sons brought a whole lot of joy to my life back then, and I would not subject them to any of the shit that I had to endure. I regularly kept in touch with my grandmother, and we often had honest conversations. I could tell she had had preconceived notions about me, possibly me being the son of her son or maybe because of the things she heard about me from my mother. I never let that deter me due to the fact that she was one of the last links to my father. We always kept in touch with each other. I had encountered so much negativity from my maternal relatives for so many years that I expected nothing less. I received gravity from outsiders for the most part and that further let me know that being disliked in the home wasn't normal, particularly being the youngest child and having done nothing against anyone in the family. I never looked for any negativity in anyone from the outside, but I acknowledged it when I saw it. Whenever I saw behavior from outsiders that reminded me of my home life, it was easy to get away from. By the fall of '92' I was back on my feet with a full time job that I would keep. I felt good knowing that I could get my sons whatever they needed, and during my time working there most of us managed to put a union together, and I was the Recording Secretary as well as the Secretary/Treasurer. I took all of the minutes at our meetings and regularly met with a CPA to make sure that the money from our dues was always correct to the penny. I was unanimously selected for those positions and I willingly accepted the responsibility. At the beginning of '93' my mother asked me if I had plans for the new year. After I told her I didn't know she said "You can get out." I got an apartment with a friend, but the funny thing is that when I was getting my belongings out of the house, my mother made sure she was in plain view wherever I went. She didn't look at me and never said a word the whole time, and when I was done I just closed the door behind me. I still went back to the house periodically and my mother was still true to her ways. If my mother and I had any conversation it was brief, but for the most part, when she saw me come into the house she would immerse herself into a puzzle book. I was happy with my children so there wasn't much that could disrupt that fact. I still displayed unconditional love towards my siblings and I always initiated the interactions we had. My oldest sister and older brother were the only ones close by. I wanted some truth as to why the family was so fucked up, but my sister blew off whatever I mentioned and my brother was clueless overall. That let me know that I couldn't get into any details about my suspicions as far as the family went. I also began to realize that anything I did mention or things they saw me do was brought to our mothers' attention. Maybe she asked as if she gave a damn or maybe they just volunteered, but I know if they always dealt with me half way in person then I shouldn't be on their mind at all if I'm not around. Working and taking care of my children helped take me away from that situation physically and mentally, however, that situation would become instrumental in the way I would bring them up. They would be united as brothers and would always look out for one another. Around that time my older brother would talk to me about a co-worker of his that he was getting serious with. He showed me a picture of her, which convinced me, the fact that he was in his mid 20's and had only been in one relationship just made me happy for him. They became married in the mid 90's and I received the invitation on short notice. I didn't make the wedding, but I had been calling her sister in law well before then. We got along pretty well, but there was an incident when I called their house to say happy birthday to her. She answered the phone and seemed pretty appreciative of the call, but I could hear my brother grumbling in the background. I could tell that she was trying to keep things calm on their end. He either didn't like the fact that I called or her appreciation for the gesture. I took it as an act of jealous insecurity on his part, but I had long realized that people will not admit when you're right about them, especially if it doesn't make them look good. I never called their house for anything after that. My mother was working at a community center in the project I was brought up in and was still living there as well. When I went to her house I was still receiving the same emotional distance, but when I went to the office where she was working, she was always engaging and smiling around her co-workers. That pattern of behavior on her part had gotten old to me by then. It had always been 'frown on me in private and smile on me in public', but I wasn't confused about it anymore. 'Sincerely phony' was what I called it. I owed it to myself to acknowledge the things that went on around me and to be mindful of other peoples' behavior. By that I didn't need any confirmation on the things I observed. It became easy to figure that when a person's words and actions don't run parallel, it pretty much makes them a hypocrite. Since my mothers' stance against me was so strong she should've let her co-workers know. My siblings knew she didn't give a damn about me, so why should anyone else matter? My sons were a pleasant distraction from bad memories and unpleasant realities as they related to the family I was born into. I saw my oldest sister and my older brother regularly, but whenever I brought up the subject of our family dysfunction and any ideas I had on it, my sister would say "That ain't it." and my brother would say "Don't dwell on the past." I couldn't afford to be in any kind of denial for the simple fact that I had been enduring that dysfunction since conception. I understood very well that ignored or forgotten history repeats itself, and I specifically remember the time that I heard my mother say "What a tangled web we weave, when we practice to deceive." That is exactly what she did, and was continuing to do. None of our interactions were purposeful or thoughtful. Many of them were meaningful, but for the wrong reasons. My oldest brother was released around the mid 90's and we hooked up when he got out. We rapped for a short time, got some drinks and ended up at our sister's house. I don't know how long we were there, but they started arguing, fussing and cussing. She told him to get out of her house and he said something back that prompted her to go after him. I held her back while he went out the door. We walked over to our mother's house from there. Our mother was verbally chastising him while we were there, and he actually didn't say anything back to her. I don't ever recall a time when he didn't respond to someone while they were talking against him. I simply looked at the expressions on both of their faces through it all, and this was new to me. I never said a word, but it made me realize that I was more familiar with her berating me in front of my older brother for nothing in particular. I don't know how it was when my brothers were in her presence, but when the three of us were in her presence she never had much to say. Around that time my oldest brother would periodically visit me where I was living at the time, and I found out that a friend of his had a job set up for him. We walked to the drug store one particular day and once we got there I told him "Things ain't the same as you remember." and he said "You know I can't keep my hand off of these white peoples' shit." He came over on the day he was supposed to start his job, and I gave him some money to go to the store so he could get change for bus fare. Within ten minutes a neighbor came to the door and informed me that he was caught stealing in the store. I walked over to the store and got his ID card. All I could say to him was "Look at you now." There was a pattern of behavior that he had been putting on display for way too long. He was the firstborn of a teenage mother, so I know he saw some less than mature behavior on her part. For as long as I could remember, he was lying, stealing and defying authority. Without ever being disciplined at home it really didn't matter where he was when he chose to be on the wrong side of the law. He and our mother were both very mean spirited, but she reserved her evil ways for the house to ensure the outside perception of her remained positive, which was far from the truth. He had no restraint and would seek to take advantage of anyone. Things were good until late '96' and I ended up staying at my mother's house again. I was sleeping on the floor or the couch; living out of my duffel bags. I was on an indefinite layoff from my job, but I got up and out every morning to do something positive for myself. Before the year was out I got a job working at the hospital and I also began taking GED classes at night. By the time I came in it was usually time to lay it down for the night. If I wanted to sleep on the couch I would have to wait for her to finish watching television and go upstairs or I could go up to the other room and find space on the floor between her office furniture. The furniture was positioned so the door would remain open, and I had to deal with it. One day around that time I was at the post office and I saw the man who was allowed to come by the house for all of those years. The man who my mother named as my older brothers' biological father without having him own up to it. We talked briefly and he gave me his phone number to give to her. When I got to the house I gave her the number without hesitation and didn't give it a second thought. I could only assume that she reached out to him and made contact because within the week I came in the back door from work and she gave me a hug and said "I love you." and that she thought she had lost contact with him for good. That was the only time in my entire life that she ever told me that she loved me, but I realized then that it wasn't about me at all. When I got by myself all I could do was shake my head. Maybe she was right in her own eyes or maybe she was unconscious in her ways. I believe she made a pact with herself to never show me any love at all. I had been going through it my whole life, and there was no exception to the rule. I was spending a lot of time at my oldest sisters' house and I saw my older brother from time to time. My older sister would visit back then, and even though we didn't write to each other or call, when we saw one another she looked at me as if she heard something bad about me and believed it. We went years at a time without seeing one another and that was my experience once we were face to face. Having a relative to say "I'm just happy to see you." was an afterthought. Family love was non-existent, and if it ever did exist it was before I was born. I only saw manipulation and deceit. The lies were obvious and the secrets were kept hidden. I was getting paid every two weeks working at the hospital while getting significantly less money than my previous job while paying child support. I received a check for $17 dollars and I was infuriated. I actually wrote a letter to the judge who ordered me to get a job that would pay me what I was getting paid at my previous job. I let my mother know what my situation was as far as the $17 check and she burst out in laughter. I could only think of when I worked overtime at my previous job and made significantly more money. I let my mother know about that and my older brother happened to be there at the time. She downplayed it to the utmost and even gave my older brother a steel look that made him keep his mouth shut. She wouldn't have a good feeling about anything I did that was positive and ultimately wanted to break my spirit and kill my will. My siblings were pawns in this game of deceit and deception, but if they did know what was going on, they still conducted themselves in accordance with our mothers' manipulation. They followed the subtle nuances, gestures and innuendo that she put on display without acknowledging the facts of the matter. They knew that my mood would be evident by the expression on my face and my mother would make sure that her demeanor would contradict my mood especially if it was positive. I was facing the reality that my mother never liked me at all, and I had the sense to know that you can't love someone if you don't even like them. She made sure that there was always an emotional distance between us, but I never outwardly reacted to it simply because I didn't trust her and I always felt she was capable of evil deeds. I was told that she poisoned my father, and I found it easy to believe by that time. She was successful at getting my siblings as well as a few other family members to see me as she did. By the summer of '97' I went back to my old job for financial reasons, and every morning I got up to go to work she would get up and go downstairs to sit in my view. She didn't have anywhere to go and she never said a word. She was going out of her way to try to make me uncomfortable and miserable, and I knew she didn't like the fact that I never confronted her about how she dealt with me. When I was a child I would cry sometimes when she was mean to me, but as I became older those tears were replaced with anger, but I never disrespected her. I was controlling my anger because even though I was pissed off plenty of times I always kept my peace. There would be times when I missed my ride to work and had to go back in the house, and I dreaded it. I simply laid down on the floor and put my thoughts in order when that happened. Sometimes I would go to my oldest sisters' house or I would get a cold beer and sit in the crack house close by. My older brother spoke with me about spending time over there and I knew that he was following up on words from our mother. She didn't like me and he didn't fuck with me for real, so I didn't take any of it seriously. When I went back to the house she said that she would take her door key if she heard about me being there again. That would simply put me in a position to spend time wherever I wanted to. My thinking was that the company I kept should not matter at all if they didn't deal with me in any capacity. That situation only took me back to a time in the early '90's when I was befriended by a guy I had never seen before. We just happened to be at the same place at the same time, and a conversation sparked up. I distinctly remember him saying that I reminded him of his brother who had recently passed. He would drive to the house after that, and I would ride out with him. We would go to a nearby neighborhood, drink beer and conversate. When it became noticeably regular my older brother came to me and said "You don't really know who this guy is for real." My older brother never dealt with me as a sibling before he made that comment and never did afterwards. By the spring of '98' I was preparing to leave town. It would hurt to leave my young sons, but I had to strive to make a better life for myself in order to make their lives better. I had never considered leaving them for good. At that time my mothers' disdain for me had become more regular and more outward, and I asked her if she had some kind of problem with me. She stepped to me chest to chest and suggested that maybe I had a problem with her. I didn't entertain that notion at all, and when I was getting my things together at the house to leave, she just stood close by while watching me go back and forth as I was gathering my things together. When I got to my last duffel bag, my mother had taken a seat in the path of my departure. She never said a word the whole time, and never looked in my direction. I thought about saying something on my way out, but I already knew that any common courtesy comments would not have been sincere. I had come to the realization that she was only waiting to close the door behind me after I left. I moved to Prince William County in Northern Virginia and tried to reestablish my life. I had to start out through various job agencies for gainful employment simply for survival until I was able to establish some stable financial means. I loaded and unloaded trucks at Frito-Lay, cleaned airplanes at Dulles Airport, and worked as a dispatcher at a dumpsite in Lorton. One job that I was willing to try was a substitute teacher. I went to different schools and the situations would be different as well. I worked in 1st grade classes, 4th grade classes, and classes for special needs children. That experience gave me an opportunity to try to understand children from the outside looking in. I also looked back on the times that I had with my four young sons and how I had to manage them. There would be times when I had my sons as well as some of my nieces and nephews all together. There would be no less than ten children at a time simply because I had to have them interact with the other children wherever we were. I had to get all of those different personalities together and get them all on a similar level in an attempt to create a consistent harmony between them all. I used that same approach when I dealt with the children in the classroom. By the time school was starting for the '98'-'99' year I received a temporary to permanent position at an elementary school as a Kindergarten Paraprofessional. The school was in Alexandria and the faculty was genuinely nice towards me. The principal and the custodian were the only other males working in the building besides me, and everyone seemed to get along with each other. I liked working with kids and it didn't take long for them to gravitate towards me. Working with them gave me a sense of purpose; I felt wanted and needed, and the fact that I could reach them and help them as well as uplift them and teach them made me feel good about myself. It actually got to the point where some of the students would run to me from the bus and give me hugs in the morning. That was a welcome change from the reality I was used to. When I did call home to keep in touch, my mother sounded as if she was happy to hear from me over the phone, but I knew better than to feed into it simply because it was quite contrary to the negative vibes I had always received from her in person. My older brother was the same way in regards to sounding happy to hear from me, but when I visited neither of them ever had much to say, and if the three of us were be broken by anyone. I was simply trying to get my life together and that was my main focus. I had long been aware of how things were when it came to the relationship between my mother and I; she never once said good morning to me and when I was young, sitting at the kitchen table doing my homework she would come in from work, look at me, look away and go to her bedroom sanctuary without saying a word. I spent a lot of years waiting and hoping for her to act like a mother to me, but at that point the truth was it was just a sad reality. I recall one time that I went to see her where she worked, and she told me about a young girl who asked her to pay for a field trip for one of my sons to go on. She justified her position by saying "And he don't come see me"... The irony in all of that was the fact that the woman who brought her own children up using only devious manipulation and divisive maneuvers while showing no love at all was holding a position of responsibility dealing with other peoples' children. She didn't have to pay his way for the field trip and it was obvious that the girl had some type of affinity towards my son at the time, but my mother never reached out to any of my children from the time any of them were born, including the entire three years when I was out of town. She never visited or called them. At that point I was basically processing information as it related to my life when it came to my blood relatives. There was one time in particular when I went to see her there and one young boy was being disrespectful by talking back to her. Her evil looks and gestures had no effect on him and he didn't flinch at all. Before too long she had made an attempt at reaching out to put her hands on him. I said to her "You can't be putting your hands on other peoples' children." The mean spirit and evil heart that I was all too familiar with was back on display. I made it a point to be mindful of the facts and be honest with myself about things of that nature. My sons had been playing recreation football since they were four and five years old, and it was time for them to start practice again. My older brother showed up at one of the first practices, but after that he never reached out or showed any more interest in his nephews. It became apparent to me that he was urged to fake his interest by our mother. I also found out that he, just as our mother never attempted to reach out to my sons the entire time that I was out of town. That was just some more information that I had to process and be mindful of. It was clearly obvious once again that he was put up to interacting with me by our mother in an attempt to make things appear regular as they applied to him and me. He simply carried out our mothers' orders when it came to dealing with me without realizing that while she was using him to help her to conspire against me, neither of them realized, or didn't care that I was watching them as well. There were many times that I had to put a question mark by his name as a brother, simply because of the loyalty factor. He looked at me through our mothers' eyes and simply followed her directions when it came to dealing with me. He didn't know how to use guile or deception when he dealt with me; he just did what our mother told him and went about his business. He only pretended to show interest when I called him on the phone, and after that football practice he never reached out to me anymore, but he would always put common courtesy on display whenever we happened to be at the same place at the same time. I knew back then that common courtesy was far from love, especially when I was dealing with a blood relative. I was learning how to detect the degree of sincerity from outsiders by the experiences I had while dealing with my own family members. I visited my oldest sister regularly, and there was always a mutual display of love put on between her children and me. I lived with my oldest sister more than a few times, and I often entertained her children when I was there. There was always open communication between us, and many times we talked in groups with everyone involved openly expressing their own opinions. Around that time my oldest brother was out of prison for one of his many brief home visits; he never stayed out for too long, but we kicked it together at my oldest sisters' sometimes. We would drink a few beers together, but his M.O. was petty theft to support his drug addiction. I had seen together our mother would still silence him with a subtle stare. They were putting their heads together against me while our mother did all of the conspiring, but it really didn't take much convincing for him to be against me. I could safely assume that he was already halfway there. Dealing with them definitely made me realize that you can't make a person like you and you can't force yourself on anyone, especially blood relatives because anyone on the outside would assume that family affinity would be automatic. Working in the school gave me an opportunity to see first-hand the love that the parents showed towards their children when they dropped them off and when they came to pick them up. I specifically noticed the affection that the mothers' showed for their sons, and I could tell that the love they showed was sincere and unconditional. I felt privileged to witness those interactions since I didn't have any experiences that were remotely similar. It was a beautiful thing to me. I made acquaintances with plenty of the parents in the interests of their children, and from that I received further insight on parent/child relationships. I was made permanent when the teacher I was working with went out on maternity leave. I worked there for the '99'-'00' school year as well, but with a different teacher. The job description was the same; I made sure the students had their necessary materials and I graded assignments. I also had to chaperone them to music, art, P.E., lunch and the library. I also took them outside for recess. The teacher I was with let me spend more time alone with the children, which gave me an opportunity to come up with my own assignments for them. I realized that guidance and positive motivation were two things that every child needed, and I did my best to get through to each and every student that I interacted with. With that first year behind me I easily settled in; I had become familiar with the faculty and staff, and I wasn't the new face anymore. The school had a different principal and added two more males to the staff, bringing the total to five. There would be times when other teachers would get on the intercom in my class and ask if I could come to their classroom and assist them with a child they may have been having trouble with; usually a young male. They almost always looked like me and I never had too much of a problem getting them to loosen up and lose their attitudes. I could tell from all the ones I had to talk to that there was probably something relevant missing from their lives, and they were just acting out. We went on field trips, and sometimes parents would chaperone, which gave us an opportunity to split the class into groups with their help. I went back home to visit before the end of the school year, and I brought my sons back with me. I took one of them to school with me each day for the last week to let them see what I was doing to earn my living. They stayed in the classroom where I worked and saw it first-hand. The teacher that I was working with at the time showed them love, and the secretary in the main office took one of them to lunch with her. Before the school year was officially over I was informed that I would be transferred to a newly built school for the '00'-'01' school year. The politics of the school system were really put on display more whereas the school I would be leaving was more close knit and family oriented. There was underlying pressure to conform to concepts and ideas that I didn't wholeheartedly agree with. The students were from a vast amount of different ethnicities, and some of them barely spoke English at all. A few of them would address me as 'Sir', and I knew that my work would be cut out for me. My focus on getting through to the students in order for them to get their lessons down was still the same, and quite honestly it was better than dealing with the faculty and staff. The teacher that I worked with was younger than I was, and she didn't have any children of her own, so we basically combined our strong points as they related to children to create a positive and progressive classroom environment. There were a few other paraprofessionals that I was familiar with from my last school as well as other substitute assignments, but no one that I could really relate to. They probably couldn't relate to me either, because I didn't know anything about adjusting my character without understanding what the benefit would be. It was better for me to work one on one with the students as much as I could simply because they were from so many different nationalities and spoke different languages. I helped them all to reach a certain level of progress by the end of the school year, and as I looked back on how they were as far as basic comprehension and understanding when the school year began it was clearly evident. At the end of the school year there were quite a few parents that came into the classroom and personally thanked me for the work that I had put in to help their children; people from all ethnicities who were only concerned with the growth of their children and not how they received it or where it came from. That was especially gratifying to me because it made me feel genuinely appreciated, and by people who didn't know me at all; it didn't matter to them. From the last half of my second year and throughout my third year of being a paraprofessional I also worked part time at Radio Shack, and I fulfilled all of the duties in the store that were expected of me including doing the inventory, locking up after closing and putting the receipts in the drop box at the bank afterwards. It was a positive experience for me and I definitely learned plenty while I was working there. I knew that after the school year was over that I would be returning to my hometown, and the main objective would be to reconnect with my sons to reestablish my relationships with them. I went back in the summer of '01' and immediately began to seek employment. I wanted to get back into the paraprofessional field, but after I found out that they were making significantly less money than I was making in Alexandria. I went to job fairs, employment agencies and the Virginia Employment Commission to find work. I landed a job in Suffolk at a business, and it started out pretty well. I ended up having to take days off to go to court because of my oldest sons' legal troubles. That job fell through in the fall of '01' and I was once again searching. I reconnected with a friend who I was working with before I left town and he helped me get a job in the freight and cargo business which I was already familiar with. Things were going well for about two months until the boss made an attempt at making a joke at my expense. I guess the unwritten rule was that if your employer says something that is supposed to be funny and laughs then you should laugh as well, but I didn't see it that way. I simply told him to his face that it wasn't funny. There was another friend of mine who was also working there, and he said to me "You know he didn't like that." I said "Fuck him." I was not going to be the one he thinks that he can shine on for everyone else's entertainment. I pretty much knew after that, my days working there were numbered. Sure enough, within two weeks after I said what I had to say to him, the boss informed me that I was no longer needed. I had to accept that fact, but within a week I received a call from one of the companies that I applied to at a job fair. I went in for an interview and took a written aptitude test, and I would also have to take a drug test, but I passed them both and started my new job in January of 2002. Having been on so many different jobs at that point in my life I knew that the main priority was getting to work on time and not missing any days, which I was certainly up to doing. I still visited my mother from time to time, and the vibe was always the same as it had been. She was working at a center in the housing project that I grew up in with children, and I thought to myself how ironic that was. When I went to see her she was always pleasant, engaging and warm hearted. That was quite the contrary to when I went to see her where she lived. That was where she openly displayed the characteristics of the mother I grew up in the same house with. She was still cold hearted and distant; always seeming to immerse herself into whatever she was doing after she saw me come through the door while showing no interest or no concern in me at all. When she was at her kitchen table doing one of her 'Fill-A-Word' puzzle books she would barely lift her head to acknowledge me, she never asked any questions and never attempted to spark up any conversation. She would always respond to anything that I said with one word or one sentence answers. By that time my anger had subsided and any confusion that I had was gone because I would not let my spirit him the same way for so long that I could basically tell what he would say or do in a given situation. I believe he felt that he had to prove something to himself for whatever reason. He had gotten himself banned from a local grocery store for stealing to support his habit. I truly believe that he did some fucked up shit to me when I was a baby, and when he became an intravenous drug user I immediately wondered how he ended up with the same affliction that my father had, because the thought of shooting drugs into my veins hadn't crossed my mind up to that point. I brought that notion up to my oldest sister, but she basically attributed his drug use to a means of dealing with his divorce. I never believed that simply because I had never seen him show any love to anything or anyone, and I truly believe in the 'balance of nature'. I had come to the conclusion that the dysfunction was here to stay due to the fact that the people in my family who started the dysfunction had no intentions of coming clean for even their own conscience. I began to realize that my oldest brother was carrying himself with me the way he did in order to find out if and what I had known or remembered. The relationship between my mother and I had long been estranged, but she knew about some of the things I was doing because of the people that I was around. The way she used to scream on me when I was a child made it very easy to be quiet around her. I learned how to keep information to myself after I realized that my voice had no significance in the house that I grew up in. Around that time an incident occurred while I was at my oldest sisters' house. I was sitting on the couch near the front door when my older brothers' wife and stepdaughter came in. They walked past me without saying a word, and since I had shown them nothing but unconditional love after meeting them I could only conclude that the family manipulation against me had reached them as well. It caught me off guard at first, but after further analysis I wasn't surprised at all. I would be honest to myself first and foremost before I would allow someone other than me dictate my mood. I realized that if I stayed true to myself I would have the opportunity to recognize when someone else was breaking character. I stayed with my oldest sister for another stint around that time and she also had a live-in boyfriend as well. Her boyfriend had a son who had access to the house as well, and there were two new outfits that I had bought and put in the hall closet with the rest of my things that ended up missing. I confronted my oldest sister about my missing clothes and she said to me "You shouldn't have brought them in here." She had never come at me that way before, but I wasn't totally surprised by what she said. I was just mad at the fact that her boyfriends' son had stolen my shit, and I wanted to balance that situation out. I haven't seen him since I found out who he was. Six months into my new job I had a transportation crisis, and I asked my mother if I could use her car to get back and forth to and from work. She reluctantly agreed, but she also never drove the car herself. After about two weeks she called me and told me to bring her keys for whatever reason, and I couldn't question it because the car belonged to her. For a while after that I had to get up in the morning an hour earlier than usual to catch a ride to work. I was basically just doing what I had to do. Not long after though, I received a blessing when a cousin of my sons had to go to California and he sold me his car. I had stable transportation, but my living arrangements were still unsettled. I was at my oldest sisters' house on one particular day when my older brother and his family came over. While they were there I made a comment that my sister in law obviously thought was funny. She was laughing aloud, and I noticed while she was laughing that my brother started coughing loudly, and acting as if he was clearing his throat while looking his wife in the eyes the whole time. The fact that he was uneasy about his wife laughing at something I said was a clear sign of insecurity as well as envy, because he didn't try to hide what he was doing at all. I could only look away and shake my head about it simply because it was a weak gesture on his part. By that time I had long been keeping mental notes as they related to my experiences with my blood relatives. I was simply trying to keep my job and do what I could for my sons. I felt betrayed by the family I grew up in the same house with, but I realized that as a grown man I couldn't act out on my feelings. Around that time I went to visit my mother at the center where she worked, and I received another wake up call. She had some school notebooks to give to me for my sons, however, she said to only give them to one of my sons in particular. Her reasoning in her own words was "Because he's the only one who acts like he got some sense." I had four sons at the time, and neither of them would ever be singled out when it came to me or anyone else providing for them. It pissed me off simply knowing that she never reached out to my children whether I was around them or not, and realizing how she dealt with her own children. There wasn't a chance of me feeding into any divisive maneuvers when it came to my sons. That was the last time I ever went to visit her. I had to endure her abuse and neglect ever since I was conceived, and when she found out that my first son was on the way she made it very clear to me that it didn't matter to her at all. I realized that she didn't even have any love for herself, and my intelligence wouldn't let me accept it anymore. "What a tangled web we weave when we practice to deceive." is something I my mother would say from time to time, and it definitely stuck with me because she was really talking about herself. I was still spending a lot of time at my oldest sisters' house, and sometimes I would confide in her about the family dysfunction. She told me that our mother had poisoned my father before he went home and died, and I believe it took a lot just for her to say that. There were times when she would look at me and say "I raised you." It wasn't far from the truth, but she probably didn't have much say in the matter because even with five children our mother was living her life as if she had none at all. My oldest sister let me know that our mother was curious as to why I stopped going to see her, but I'm pretty sure knew that our mother never wanted me to be born, and never acted like she gave a damn about me after I was. It wasn't long before my oldest sister let me know that our mother wanted her door key from me, and I relinquished it willingly.

That simply let me know she felt as though she was well within her rights to not give a damn about me. After that I made a point to never mention my mothers' name to my oldest sister again for the simple fact that I knew she couldn't be impartial to the both of us. Around May '04' I got an apartment, and it was long overdue just because I was always around somebody at their place. I never had any problem being by myself, and I was having serious trust issues as well. I really didn't know who, if anyone was in my corner, but I definitely trusted me. My older brother came by a couple of times, and his level of conversation immediately let me know that he only came by at our mothers' urging. He was talking to me about being a sitting duck; I guess he was making a reference to me being the apartment alone, but it was basically the same thing I said to him after he was threatened by the female years ago. After that second visit he didn't come again and didn't call me either. I fully realized that I had more enemies in the family that I was born into than people I came across at random. He had taken the bait from our mother once again by listening to her talk about me as if I had some type of deficiency. He wanted that to be true, but if there was anything wrong with me it was done by her. She could easily make him think something was wrong with me without having to actually say what it was, and it gave him a 'hollow confidence' simply because there was no substance to his logic. He never considered the fact that she just liked me less than she liked him, and he was easy to manipulate simply because he craved attention. When we were growing up together and I did or said anything to dispel any notion that I had any shortcomings he would always be quiet. That's when he was reminded of his own inadequacies. He never had a kind word for me on purpose. I still visited my oldest sisters' house and kicked it with my nieces and nephews when she wasn't there. Being by myself provided me with an opportunity to reflect on as much of the past as I could remember as it related to me in the present time. Laying alone at night I had quite a few visions; images flashing in front of my mind's eye. There were always five people in these visions; both of my grandmothers, my parents and my maternal aunt. The significance of my aunt was due to my mother telling me that my father and my aunt had been intimate. The significance of my maternal grandmother is the fact that she had my mother by a married man. I met him and his wife when we went to Maryland years ago, and I asked my mother how he was her father, and she gave me a mean ass look of disgust without saying a word. I remember my maternal grandmother giving me that same look many years ago when I was very young, and never talked to me. She had two daughters, my mother and my aunt, but my aunt had a dark complexion and it wasn't hard for me to figure out that my grandmother had used their obvious physical differences against them in their upbringing, especially since that was the basic method my mother used in bringing up her own children. My paternal grandmother definitely knew more than she told me about my fathers' death, and when I confronted her about it around that time she simply quoted the scriptures, saying that "Hell hath no fury like a woman scorned." I don't know if she felt like her son deserved to die, but she sounded as if she understood the situation. I believe he promised to marry my mother instead of dismissing the notion outright because he was aware of her evil capabilities, and it was quite possible that I could have had an 'accidental death' back then. Not long after my father died my mother would make flavored freeze cups and have me take them to my grandmother, and if she cooked on Thanksgiving or Christmas she would always send my grandmother some of whatever she prepared. During that time I happened to cross paths with my youngest sister by my father. The first time I saw her I was nine years old, and we were five years apart. The next time I saw her after that I was about twenty. We were both adults, and I began to run down some of the things I had been going through with my mother and she told me a story of her own. She said something about my mother staring at her when she was very young. She said "It was just the way she looked at me.", and that my mother never said a word. She also said that she cried about it after she went home. In my estimation she had no reason to make it up and I had no reason to dispute it because I was all too familiar with that look my sister was trying to describe. My mother and my oldest brother were openly mean towards children, and babies would instinctively cry aloud in the presence of my oldest brother. Those were two of the first red flags that I picked up on when it came to them. Before my sister and I went our separate ways she gave her mothers' phone number. She was also my stepmother, and I called her up. We talked for a while and I kept in touch with her without letting too much time go by between calls. In fall of '04' there was a woman at my job who had shown an obvious interest in me. She got the message across through another coworker and we soon exchanged numbers. I had some child support issues that came up which put my apartment in jeopardy. When I brought it up to my sister she told me I could stay with her, so I got one of my nephews to help me get my things out of the apartment. I stayed there a few months while still keeping in touch with my stepmother. I regularly talked on the phone with my female coworker; we were both basically trying to obtain a certain level of understanding. Before too long my stepmother told me that I could stay with her until I got myself together, and I took her up on it. During that time I was reminded that I didn't know how to fully interact with her simply because I didn't know what a normal mother and son relationship was. I definitely treated her respectfully and basically stayed out of the way, but we did have more than a few one on one conversations. My stepmother showed me unconditional love and told me things that could be beneficial to me as far as making progress in life. She told me that she loved me and basically provided me with an opportunity to further my development as an adult. During one of our conversations I told her that my father chose the right woman to marry. I told her about some of the abuse that I had to endure from my birth mother and even though she downplayed it I know she heard every word I said. At one point she began to profess to me that she never knew that my father was an intravenous drug user. She said that she only realized it in hindsight. More than once she said "I didn't know!" The tone of her voice and the look in her eyes were sincere to me, and I never thought of trying to dispute what she said. What made me wonder was why my mother would feel scorned about not getting married to an intravenous heroin user, because I sincerely believe that she knew about it. I looked at it as my mother wanting a husband to put her burdens on so she could continue living her life as she pleased. I was my fathers' only child by my mother and he would have had his work cut out for him had he chosen to marry her. He knew that way better than I did, but even as a young child, I never saw her turn down male attention. When I was living in my apartment my oldest sister informed me that our mother wanted me to submit my address to whomever was involved with my oldest brothers' incarceration due to the fact that he was about to be released from penitentiary. I gave no response to it at all because now my mother was trying to get to me through my oldest sister after she only wanted her door key when she realized I wouldn't visit her anymore, and it was on the behalf of the only child of hers' that I had ever seen her give a sincere smile to. I realized that they made a choice to be half minded, and the only way I could relate to them was to be mean spirited, hard hearted and selfish. Those ingredients were never present in my character. I continued to stay in touch with my female friend from work, and things were cool because I wasn't about playing any games or any other bullshit simply due to prior experiences. We were hitting it off pretty well just because in most relationships everyone is always on their best behavior in the beginning. We spent time together, and I must have called her from my sisters' house prior, because one time I was at her house my nephew called there for me. It made me feel good because I realized that he made a sincere gesture towards me, and he let me know that he valued the times and experiences that we shared together. My female friend and I were feeling closer, and when we finally consummated our relationship she became pregnant. She made it clear to me that she didn't want another child, but I pleaded against it. I even told her that I would take the baby, but she still went through with the abortion. When I saw her at work after that she walked right past me without acknowledging me at all, so I had it in my mind that it was the end of us. I mentioned the situation to my oldest brother and he replied without hesitation "I know you're not going to mess with her anymore." I received an instant revelation from that comment, and I realized that she had done no more wrong to me than the people that I grew up in the same house with, and they're my blood relatives who I basically had to interact with my entire life. I didn't approve of the abortion and I was more disappointed about it than I was angry. I went on working and going about my business in an effort to move on. I was at my oldest sisters' house, and we were in the dining area talking when the phone rang. My sister answered it, and she handed the phone to me with a certain expression on her face. I could tell that it was about to be something different, and it was. My female friend called for me to basically let me know that she wanted us to continue seeing one another. I wasn't against it at all, and it provided me with an opportunity to let her know where I was coming from. I let her know a little about how I came up and some of the things that I had to endure from my own family, and that she hadn't done me any worse than they did. I also let her know that I understood her point of view. I ultimately looked at it as a test of forgiveness because my blood relatives would always be that, but she and I didn't have to face each other again. There were people putting their heads together against me for as long as I could remember, and I call them family. Around that time I made one final attempt at getting closer to the truth about some family history. I told my oldest sister that I believed that our oldest brother ended up with the same affliction that my father had because he sodomized me when I was a baby. My eyes were closed in that recurring memory, but I truly believe that's what happened. She replied once again, "That ain't it." I began to believe that she knew what 'it' was. I realized that I would get no further than I had gotten up to that point and left it alone while always observing, recognizing and acknowledging any signs or symptoms of dysfunction whenever I interacted with my siblings. I focused on my job, my relationship and stabilizing my life. I left my stepmothers' house and moved in with my female friend around that time, and we were both putting all we had into giving the relationship every chance to grow. My oldest brother was still back and forth in and out of jail, and he was out for another visit around that time, but unlike before I didn't make any attempts to reach out to him. It must have made him feel a certain way about it because a mutual friend of ours relayed his profanity-laced tirade regarding the situation to me. He had never meant me any good, and he was only playing the brother role as a double agent; waiting for me to say something that he could relay to our mother. Time was moving on and around the fall of '06' my female friend became pregnant again. We had been living together for a while and I guess she made a different decision this time regarding her pregnancy based on the way she felt about our situation being together. We lived in different places while being together, but I had always made myself accessible to my sons. During the school year I would have them over on some weekends, and during the summer I would have them over to the house a little more. They were old enough to ride on the bus then, so when it was time for them to go back home I would walk with them to the bus stop, and we all talked until the bus came. I told my older brother about having another son on the way, but he was no more receptive than he had ever been with me about anything. My oldest sister was a little more receptive, but she was probably thinking about the outcome of the first pregnancy. I was only thankful that I could recognize and realize things then. Our son was born on May 29, 2007; exactly two weeks after my birthday. Around that time I was also in the process of changing my last name to my fathers' last name. I was told as a child that he named me in the hospital shortly after I was born, but on my Birth Registration Card my mothers' last name was at the end; after my fathers' last name.

I wanted her last name dropped for obvious reasons. My relationship with her was strictly conditional, and all of the conditions came from her. His last name is the one thing that he left me for sure, and even though he's not here I could keep the name going that goes back to WWII. The combination of my upbringing and the family that I grew up with made it an easy decision. My youngest son would have the last name, and his brothers could change their last name if they chose to do so. I mentioned it to my oldest sister and before too long my oldest brother was making a comment about it from jail. One of my nephews told me that my oldest brother asked what the fuck was wrong with me for changing my last name. I had the mindset that if I didn't interact with you on a personal level then your name would not be coming out of my mouth. That piece of information traveled from my oldest sister to my mother to my oldest brother in a very short period of time, so it was quite obvious that they didn't have any problem mentioning my name. Around that time my oldest sister relayed a message to me from my mother pertaining to a life insurance policy. I heard her out, but I didn't put it at the top of my priority list. She made it her business to remind me more than a few times, saying that I had to sign some papers so the money wouldn't go to the state. One day shortly after that reminder I went to the office after work and signed the paperwork without fully knowing what it was about. I gave it a second thought after the fact, but it was already done. I would still visit my oldest sister, and sometimes my older brother and his family would be there. Things were a lot different from my end simply because I knew that he was a victim of devious manipulation and had gotten his ways towards me across to his family. The fact that I had done nothing against him or his family didn't matter at all, and I knew that even though our oldest brother was always antagonizing him while we were growing up he always wanted some type of acceptance from him. I was at a friends' house around that time when I realized that where he lived was just minutes away from my older brother. When my friend and I were done vibing I called him to say that I was coming through. When I got there I witnessed another display of sincere fakeness. Our conversation was general common courtesy which had nothing to do with our relationship with each other. He offered me a drink of Hennessy and I accepted, but when I picked my drink up, I noticed that he was motioning to his son while pointing at me with a certain expression on his face, and his son; my nephew, reacted as if he had picked up on some classified information. There was silence a few times, but he was telling me everything without saying a word. After a while, out of the blue, he said "Call me when you get home." He was basically letting me know that he wanted me to leave his house, and I did. Neither he nor his family stopped for one second to realize that I had done nothing against any of them, but I could easily tell that the narrative in regards to me had spread to some of my other nieces and nephews. I guess they fed into the narrative that if anyone who had an estranged relationship with their mother had to be responsible for it. I also knew that it's never good to act or speak out of ignorance; the less you know, the less input you should have. I had pretty much become numb in regards to my oldest brother simply because I realized that he didn't know any other way to be, but on occasion I would visit my oldest sister and she would have a one page letter to me from him. Around that time I received a call from my older sister, who I hadn't seen or heard from in years. How I was doing or what I was going through wasn't even an issue; she was calling for some money. I agreed to send her what she asked for and she continued to talk at length about some of the things that were going on in her life. I didn't rush at all when it came to sending the money to her, and I guess after enough time had passed where she felt that she should have received it I began to receive frequent calls from her. Since I already knew why she was calling I never even bothered to pick up, but she left several angry messages on my phone, and even accused me of lying to her. I did send the money though, and I was quite sure she received it because the calls from her stopped. Plenty of time passed before I heard from her again, but her reason for calling was all off. Her son; my nephew gave me a call late one night to let me know that he was in town. He was at my oldest sisters' house, but I was in for the evening and didn't go back out that night. She talked plenty of shit to me about not wanting to see him and hung the phone up after she was finished talking. I just listened without responding because just as did with my mother and my other siblings I let her show me who she was and how she was. The call was unwarranted and unjustified due to the fact that she never checked on me when she came into town, and her children had only come to see me once when they were in town. I usually found out from one of my oldest sisters' children after they were already gone, but I also found out that they visited my older brother every time they did come. The relationship between my lady and me was not without its ups and downs, but our love and commitment to each other was, and still is there. Around that time the subject of marriage was coming up more frequently between the both of us. I felt that having a newborn son provided me with a single purpose as well as stability, and I was ready for the total commitment. At the beginning of '09' we went to the Marriage Commissioners' Office inside the City Hall Building and got it done. My oldest sister and future mother in law were our witnesses. I still checked up on my oldest sister, and I thanked her for never being totally like our mother and other siblings. I was hoping to find out some new information regarding our family dysfunction, but at that point we were just extending common courtesy towards each other. She would let me know about some things that were going on between her and our mother, but at that point I was only listening due to the fact that I already knew that people talk to the person that they talk about, and I didn't feel that she should say anything about me to our mother simply because she knew first-hand about the relationship we had. Our conversations were getting shorter, but there was nothing personal about it, and I was basically locked in on the family thing. My circle had gotten much smaller as far as the people that I dealt with, which was and still is a good thing. My two sons who were just above my baby boy had graduated from high school around that time, I was happy about that without question. I was trying to understand them from the outside looking in, and I told them to finish high school at least to make their mom feel proud. I wouldn't say they did it for me and won't take any credit for them graduating; I'm just happy that it was something that they accomplished. I simply let them know that real life experiences would be directly up the road. A short while after we were married my wife threw me a surprise birthday party. She enlisted the help of three of my sons to do it, and I must admit that I was pleasantly surprised. There were dozens of coworkers there, and all of my in laws who were in town; they actually prepared all of the food. My wife invited the very short list of my oldest and closest friends. It was a very big turnout simply because there were more people there than I could have imagined, and the way all of those people came together and contributed on my behalf made it easily the most love that had ever been extended to me in my entire life. It was the first time that so much outside affection had been directed towards me. It was something that I had no first-hand experience with, especially from so many people. I fell in and joined the party nevertheless. It wasn't too long after the party that my wife began looking for a real estate agent to begin the process of finding a family home. We looked around Virginia Beach at first simply because that's where we both worked, but we eventually agreed on a house that we both found in Norfolk. It wasn't very far from the house that I grew up in, and it was even closer to my oldest sisters' house. We visited my oldest sister prior to moving in the house, and my wife was urging me to tell her that we had found a house, but I was planning on telling her after we actually moved in. My wife couldn't resist the urge and told her anyway. My sister appeared to be very happy for us, and thanked my wife for bringing me back to Norfolk. We invited her over once we got settled in, and we basically just talked about things. We were still getting acclimated to our new surroundings as well as enjoying our privacy, but one evening in particular we were upstairs pretty much ready to call it a night when we heard the doorbell ring. When I went to answer the door it was my oldest sister, but she had my older brother and his wife with her as well. I was totally caught off guard, and to be honest I couldn't even hide it. I had told my oldest sister that he sold me out as a brother years ago so her making a conscious effort to bring him around me was beyond my comprehension. While they were there we basically interacted with each other by means of common courtesy and general conversation. There weren't even any old memories that we could bring up and laugh about due to the fact that he was brought up to believe that I was inferior to him without even entertaining the idea that our mother coached him up and regularly belittled me; especially when she felt that she had an angle to play from. He was definitely a pawn in the game that our mother was playing with her children, and either he didn't realize it or it didn't matter to him as long as he was the one who appeared to be better than me in whatever capacity. I could tell that since we were teenagers he embraced being favored over me by our mother, and I really believe that he thinks it makes him better than me in some sort of way as if we weren't all blood relatives. I was the youngest child in the family, and I had grandchildren so when I looked at my siblings from the outside I could only assume one or two things; that they were happy having someone other than them that our mother could look down on or they knew that our home life was fucked up, and were afraid to be honest with themselves about it. I had come to the realization that my mother, oldest brother and I were the only ones fully aware of just how deep the dysfunction was. Around that time I received a call from my oldest sister informing me that there was a letter at her house for me from my oldest brother. I could only assume that he and my mother put their heads together in some capacity before he wrote it, because he started it out with words suggesting there be peace between me and my mother. He also wrote in the letter that she worshiped the ground I walked on. I didn't know what his reasoning was for writing the letter at all, but I wrote a letter of my own and sent it to him. I simply let him know about things that I remembered from years ago. I let him know that I recall him sodomizing me when I was a baby, and about him waking up in the middle of the night on numerous occasions to fondle our sisters while they were asleep. I also let him know that our mother didn't give a damn about me and neither did he. I ended the letter by letting him know that it would be the last contact that we have from my end. He wrote another letter back to me denying everything that I had reminded him of, but he did go on about my father and said in the letter that he treated my mother like a punching bag. I figure if there was any truth to that, then it was their justification for not giving a damn about me at all. It also made me really believe that she had a hand in my fathers' death. I thought back to the day it happened, and the facial expression that my brother had. I was also just 'part of the room' when I heard him say "He ain't my daddy." I did go to my oldest sisters' 50th Birthday Party, and there were plenty of people there. I mingled with my nieces and nephews, along with a few neighbors and some cousins, but since I was in the know I basically dealt with my wife and son. I realized that common courtesy among relatives was about as phony as it could get, so there was no sense in laughing and joking with anybody there that I knew felt indifferent towards me. I made sure that I stayed in touch with my grandmother on a regular basis, and even though she was approaching 90 years old her mind was still keen. She told me about how my parents met and ended up together. She gave me an ID Card with my fathers' picture on it as well as some old pictures and a letter written to her by my father years ago. She also told me that she asked my mother what was wrong with me and that my mother said "I don't know." There was a blank expression on my face plenty of times as a young child, but I guess my mother didn't want to tell her that I was being neglected, abused and ignored. In the summer of '11' I started my son in recreation football just as I had done with his older brothers. It kept me occupied mentally and physically.

That would be our family thing on Saturdays in the fall. I still kept in touch with my oldest sister and the visits were becoming more brief. I had serious trust issues simply because my blood relatives never actually said to me that they didn't give a damn about me, but they definitely let me know. I was still holding out hope that one of them would actually come clean about it. One time I was at my oldest sisters' house and I said to her that this family is dysfunctional. She responded by saying that our mother did it. I guess everyone accepted it and bought in except me, and it's probably the reason I'm viewed as the black sheep of the family, the outcast or whatever one might call it. It was approaching the end of '12' and I saw one of my nephews. He told me that my oldest brother was about to be released again. The thing that struck me was while I was still visiting my oldest sister regularly she never mentioned a word about it. I knew it had something to do with the letters that she gave me from him, and I knew that when he did get out he would be staying at her house because even though he is the pick of all my mothers' children she didn't want him living with her because she was the person he got his ways from. She never disciplined him because she's the one who taught him how to lie and steal. They were and still are bound together by dark secrets, and they both had dirt on each other. When I knew that my brother was out I made a conscious decision never to go to my sisters' house again to avoid any further confusion when it came to my blood relatives. At the beginning of '13' I received a phone call from my oldest sister, but I never answered it. She left a message saying that she was worried about me, and then she went in another direction; telling me not to include her in the group of people that I had decided to distance myself from. From the tone of her voice she sounded upset, but when my wife and I moved in we gave her door keys and the security code. I felt like she could have come by if it was that serious, but me not picking up the phone was all it took for her to let loose in a message. That was very different for her, especially since she had long been accustomed to me reaching out to her. She was regularly interacting with people who didn't give a damn about me, and I knew that she couldn't be impartial from both sides. I decided to stay away from all of my siblings. Around that summer I went to a nearby convenience store and while I was at the cash register I noticed my oldest brother on the outside looking in, and then he walked around to the side of the store. I don't know if he realized that I saw him or not, but I'm definitely sure he relayed that information to our mother. The woman with the junior high school education who learned how to manipulate and deceive to damn near perfection while pretending to be humble at the same time. She was physically attractive and I know that she received plenty of male attention; probably starting from when she was a young age. Starting in 1958 she had a child approximately every 21 months by a different man, ending in 1968 with me. She could quickly take on any mood that she wanted to be in. There were many times I saw her smiling while she was outdoors and quickly frowning once she came inside. I believe she covered her shame with anger, and by rearing her five children according to their obvious differences, there would be no unity at all. She dealt with each of us individually, and I believe that whatever she said to each of us was something different. Boy, girl, girl, boy, boy; we didn't look alike, act alike or think alike and that made it that much easier for her to deal with us. We would have to come to her, but never more than one of us at a time. Those divisive maneuvers were put in place for a reason; we would never collectively come to her and question her choices as a teenager and young adult because they would be questions that she wouldn't want to answer. It's obvious that my oldest brother saw her during her most immature time as a parent, and I'm pretty sure it had a lot to do with the reason he was never disciplined for any of his wrongdoings. It was if he knew something about her that she couldn't take back, but definitely didn't want anyone else to know. I'm pretty sure my oldest sister saw some things as well since she was younger than my brother by less than two years. Even though my mother was never very nice to my older sister when we all were young, my sister basically accepted it, and always treated our mother with respect. There was one particular time when our mother was going out with one of her male friends and my older sister was pleading with her to stay for fear that our oldest brother would harm her. My mother and oldest brother looked at each other, and they were both smiling. He had physically assaulted her before so she had good reason to do what she was doing. Our mother would not be deprived of her evening entertainment and proceeded out the door. My older brother will forever be oblivious to anything that doesn't involve him directly simply because that's what our mother instilled in him. There was a time when he and I were with our mother at the house of one of her male friends and my mother had my older brother feeling so good about himself that he began dancing in front of that strange man while smiling the whole time. As usual I just acknowledged what I had seen. When we were young I recall him saying "I don't know who my daddy is.", but I could easily match the face with the name my mother gave the receptionist years ago. He was married, and my mother even had pictures of his children in her bedroom in frames. She put whatever they had together over that man owning up to his son, but in retrospect I believe they came to some kind of understanding because he knew she would not sit still waiting for him to come back around. I guess they agreed to live an honest lie. When it came to me, the youngest child, there was something different. My grandmother told me about my oldest brother going to places where my father would be for the purpose of showing his report card, and she also told me that he let my mother know that he had women. In her words, the women just had to have some of Mr. Wesley. When I think of the stories that I've heard about my father and seeing my mother in real time, I can only conclude that I was conceived by two attractive people who were more than willing to fulfill their lustful desires, and fulfill the desires of others as well. I also believe that they were into accepting romantic challenges and matching wits more than anything emotional as far as a relationship goes. Neither of them won anything, but I guess somebody at least had to feel like they had the 'ups' in whatever was going on between them. After my father died there was me, and I guess every time that my mother looked at me she saw him without realizing we were two different people, and since her other children saw me as she did they seemed to disregard the fact that was the youngest of us all. I wondered how a woman with children by five different men could really feel scorned, but I quickly realized that there would be no sense in it. Whatever she felt she took it out on me, and my oldest brother was so caught up in the things he was doing that it didn't matter to him at all. He played brother only in an attempt to gain my confidence. My oldest sister had no choice but to have me in her care, and I knew that she would never come clean 100% to me about things, but I was just glad that she was never openly mean towards me. My older sister was pretty oblivious to the family reality, and with all of the time she spent in Maryland at a young age away from the obvious dysfunction, what our mother told her was all she had to go by as far as the family situation went. My older brother is just a brother in title only simply because we never had a bond. In retrospect I now know that while I was thinking that we were close and feeling good about our relationship he had other things on his mind, specifically all the negative words he heard our mother used to describe me. It's quite natural for the older child to have most experiences before the younger child, but he was led to believe that I would never catch up to speed. The abuse and neglect that I endured back then seemingly had me going in that direction, but I sincerely believe being left handed and thinking differently from everyone else aided in my development. My observations were gradually beginning to come together, and it was starting to look like none of them knew any other way to be while I was slowly evolving. As I was getting older and began making positive strides in life as well as in school, the things that my older brother heard about me, and wanted to stay true orever, were being contradicted. Those were things our mother never prepared him for, and if I did something so basic as tackle him in a game of football or make a nice pass over him on the basketball court his response, or lack thereof, told me all I needed to know about the kind of brother he was and still is. In his mind, there are a lot of things that I'm just not supposed to know, and every time I did or said something that was contrary to what he thought about me, he created separation between us. In essence, he never attempted to get to know me for himself, and his best effort at it was taking our mother at her every word when it came to me. The family dysfunction was openly accepted by my mother and oldest brother, and it seems as if my oldest sister was just out voted, but I don't believe my older sister and brother were even aware of the concept of dysfunction. They all had their own reasons for being silent about things back then; masking guilt, going with the flow and being oblivious to the facts. As we got older I noticed a lot of pretending going on; fake smiles and such as if things were normal, but the dysfunction was still present, and the effects of incidents past were still lingering. As even more time went by I realized that coming clean about things was totally out of consideration when it came to my mother and oldest brother. My oldest sister was dealing with it in her own way, and I guess she came to the realization that history cannot be changed. By that time she had her own family, and I made it a point to commend her on raising her children as a unit as opposed to individually like our mother did with us. My older sister and brother have kept pressing forward and haven't openly mentioned anything of the dysfunction that we were brought up in; from lack of knowledge, lack of concern, or a little of both. Little do they know the effects still linger, especially when you try to downplay it, and that history you choose to pretend never existed usually repeats itself. They both have a biological son and daughter, but the way that they deal with their own children let me know that my nieces and nephews by them were and still are affected by the dysfunction as well. Watching how our mother dealt with her own children in real time, it became inherent in them and repeated itself in certain situations. Being aware of the facts only made me try to be a better person. I know first-hand how it feels to be dealt with in a totally negative way; as a child and by my mother and siblings no less, but I'm very thankful that I didn't and still don't deal with anyone the way that I was dealt with. The memories and the anger from not really being able to do anything about the mistreatment do recur at times, but I do my best to keep it under control, simply because I definitely know where any anger that I do have inside of me could be directed. Having a normal family life gives me more reasons to be happy nowadays, and that's what I want to continue. In the summer of '15' my mother passed away and we were all seeing each other on a regular basis shortly after because we all got together to clean out her house. I was hearing things from my oldest sister in regards to some furniture that I was supposed to get, but my older sister came and got it, and took it back to Maryland. I was also told that my older sister was of the opinion that I shouldn't receive anything, possibly because I had distanced myself from our mother altogether. There were plenty of nice things in the house, but I didn't want any of it; I was just helping out. When we got up to her bedroom I saw the same .25 revolver that I had given to my older brother back in the early 90's. My oldest sister let me know that my older brother and his wife were trying to get things out of our mothers' house to give to people they know where they live. It came to me as if they were trying to do a good charity deed, but I just wondered what they would have done if our mother was still alive. During the process of getting everything out of the house I interacted with my oldest brother and sister the most. I reached out to my older sister when we crossed paths, but I could tell that she wasn't really being receptive. When I saw my older brother and his wife I spoke and left It at that. My oldest sister found the insurance policies and passed them out to us. I got the figure on how much my policy was worth, and it seemed pretty low for how long she had it. It immediately let me know that it had something to do with the paperwork I signed a few years back. I wasn't mad about it; I just had to face the fact that even nearing

70 years old, my mother still had it in her to be that way and she enlisted the aid of my oldest sister to carry out her evil deed. I brought it up to my oldest sister and she had no response. Even before that revelation I was contemplating not going to the funeral. On the day of the funeral my father in law called my wife to find out where it would be, and my sister on my fathers' side called me to let me know that she would be coming in my support. I called my grandmother and she told me that I should go by all means. I got myself together to go, and my wife came to support me all the way like she had always done and still does. I didn't sit with the rest of the family, but my youngest sister came and sat beside me. When we all went outside I distinctly remember my oldest sister telling me that she was glad that I came, and my oldest brother telling me that he never stopped loving me. My older sister still had her distance on display for whatever reason, but I definitely understood that it wasn't a celebration. I went back home and stayed away like I was already doing, but before too long my oldest nephew from my oldest sister reached out to me and informed me about comments being made in regards to me when I showed up at the church. He made a point to let me know about a derogatory comment made by my older sisters' son. It simply let me know that the intentional dysfunction was still alive and well. I still continued to prioritize family and work, but around '19' my grandmother called me to come see her, and when I got there she informed me that my youngest sister had passed away. I spent time with my stepmother for support, and I also have a niece from my sister. I reached out to them when time permitted, but they were and will always be in my thoughts and prayers. In the beginning of last year I lost my grandmother to COVID 19, and later last year I lost my oldest brother to heart failure. It's present day February '22' and I'm still committed to making a better life for my family while counting my blessings and being honest with myself…PEACE!

www.ingramcontent.com/pod-product-compliance
Lightning Source LLC
LaVergne TN
LVHW041633070526
838199LV00052B/3341